MORE BOOKS BY PARKER GREY

Boss Me Dirty
An Office Romance

School Me Dirty
A College Romance

Ride Me Dirty
A Cowboy Romance

Rule Me Dirty
A Royal Romance

Double Dirty Mountain Men
An MFM Ménage Romance

Double Dirty Royals
An MFM Ménage Romance

Finding His Princess

Parker Grey

ISBN: 1974038378
ISBN-13: 978-1974038374

Chapter One

Ella

I close the back door to the diner as softly as I can, glancing at the clock on the wall as I do.

7:03. *Crap.*

Holding my breath, I tiptoe along the back hall to the tiny break room. My white sneakers just *barely* squeak on the tile floor, but even that noise makes me nervous.

Three minutes wouldn't be a big deal at any other job, but my boss Kyle is a total jerk. And worse, he's a total jerk who *lives* to brown-nose my stepmother — and catching me doing something wrong is a great way to score points with her.

The lights are on in the break room, but there's no one there, and I exhale, pushing my blonde hair out of my face as I hang my purse on a hook, grabbing my apron. It's kind of gross right now, since yesterday morning I had a table with two kids who got into a mustard fight, and I really need to take it home to wash it but just forgot yesterday, I was so tired.

I grab that, tie it around my waist, and pin my name tag on my Tremaine Diner t-shirt.

Then I take a deep breath, wind my hair into a bun, and head out to see whether we've got customers yet.

"You're late, girl," Flynn calls the moment he sees me.

"Barely!" I protest.

He puts one hand on his hip and tilts his head back so he can look down his nose at me.

"Three minutes late is still late," he says, making his voice high-pitched and nasal. "That's another demerit."

"Kyle's going to catch you doing your impression of him one of these days," I say, typing my apron strings around my back.

Flynn grins and turns his attention back to flipping pancakes.

"Not today," he says, and winks at me. "But you owe me. I covered for your pretty little butt a few minutes ago already."

"Thanks," I say. "I'm sorry, Peyton couldn't find her mascara this morning, and then Slade had a zit and broke a coffee mug, so I had to clean all that up before I came."

Flynn purses his lips and looks at the grill disapprovingly without saying anything, and I sigh.

"I know, I know, it's ridiculous," I say.

"*They're* ridiculous," he says. "Grown-ass women who pitch hissy fits when they can't find their shitty drugstore mascara and it's somehow your fault? Girl, you have *got* to get yourself out of there."

"You can say that again," I mutter.

"I'd take you up on the easy joke but you've already got a table waiting," he says. "The four-man hangover party at table seven."

I lean back, away from the window, and catch a glimpse of a few guys who look like they're still wearing what they wore to last night's black-tie event. I raise one eyebrow. People who attend black tie events aren't exactly our usual clientele.

"They *must* be hungover to eat here," I tease Flynn.

"Hey now," Flynn says. "I am a damn *expert* in hangover cures, especially for hot men who know how to dress."

Flynn winks at me.

"I thought you and Thomas were a *thing* now," I say, prying.

"Can't I have a little fun?" Flynn asks, monitoring some eggs. "Go get their order, I've got work to do."

"They have menus already?"

"Sure do."

I walk over to table five — the darkest table in the place, which they probably requested — pulling my notepad out of my pocket as I do.

"Hi there," I begin. "I'll be your server this morning. Can I start you off with—"

"Coffee," the first guy on the right side of the table growls. "Make it fast and just leave the damn pot."

I glance down at the rude bastard, making sure I don't let annoyance register on my face. He's slouching in his chair, one hand on the table and the other slung over the back, wearing a tuxedo that he's *clearly* had on since last night.

It's untucked and wrinkled, his bowtie undone around his neck. The shirt is unbuttoned just far enough that I can see the curves and contours of his thick, muscled chest.

I stare for just a moment too long, because even though he's obviously kind of a hungover jerk, he's also kind of hot in a jerk way.

Then he finally looks up at me, one eyebrow raised. "Well?" he asks.

Oh my *gosh*, he's good-looking. Even though he clearly had a pretty rough night, he's got deep slate-gray eyes, mussed hair, and exactly the right amount of stubble on his square jaw.

Not to mention, he looks kind of familiar. I could almost swear that I know him from somewhere, except I'd remember anyone this incredibly handsome. Right?

My mouth comes slightly open, and it's a moment before I remember that I'm supposed to answer.

"Of course," I say.

He's a total jerk, I think. *A complete and total jerk. Don't give him the satisfaction of thinking he's hot.*

"Could I get a Bloody Mary?" his friend says, finally snapping me out of my hot-jerk induced reverie.

"Sorry," I say, finally remembering to smile. "We don't serve alcohol."

"No alcohol? None at all?"

I shake my head.

"The cook doesn't even have a bottle of vodka stashed somewhere for the really tough mornings?"

I'm sure Flynn does, but I'm not offering it to these guys.

"I don't think so," I say as sweetly as I can, tilting my head to one side. "Orange juice?"

"Fine."

I turn to the third guy.

"I'll just take the coffee and hope for the sweet release of death," he says.

I nod.

"Same," the last guy says, not even looking up at me.

"I'll be right back with those," I say, and turn.

"Make sure it's strong," says the first guy — the hot jerk — and I glance back at him. "None of this usual diner coffee bullshit."

We lock eyes for a split second, and then his gaze travels down my body, from my head to my feet and back up as he smirks.

A jolt of electricity slams through my core, my

nerves crackling with sudden heat while this *jerk* looks me over, up and down, like I'm something he can *have*.

I stand my ground, notepad in hand, even though I can feel my face getting red.

"I'll see what I can do," I say, and walk back to the kitchen.

Chapter Two

Grayson

I lean forward as our waitress disappears, tracking her ass with my eyes until she disappears around the corner.

It's a *nice* ass, the kind of ass I can just imagine bending over a table in front of me as I slide my cock along the cleft between her cheeks. Hell, it wouldn't be the first time I went for breakfast after a big night and had a side of pussy with my eggs and toast.

And this girl? Blonde and blue-eyed, lush red lips, and she's got this rosy-cheeked innocence thing going on that I'd fucking *love* to ruin.

"Earth to Grayson," Beckett mutters. "Could you stop staring at the waitress for one fucking second?"

"I'm sure you were saying something *really* important," I say, my eyes still lingering on the spot where she disappeared.

"More important than you thinking about getting

6

your dick wet," he says, glaring at me from his chair. "Give it five minutes off, man."

My head pounds, and my mouth feels like it's being scrubbed with cotton balls dipped in acid, but I grin at him anyway, even though I'm pretty sure I look like hell.

"No rest for the wicked," I say.

The three of them all roll their eyes.

"This weekend," Beckett's best friend, Kieran, says. "The World Cup. In Florence. You two coming or what?"

Next to me, Declan groans and rubs two hands over his eyes.

"After last night, I'm taking up a life of baking cupcakes and watching soap operas," he says, and we all laugh.

"Hell yes, we're coming," I say, sneaking one more glance at the corner where the waitress disappeared. Now I'm thinking about the way she just barely pursed her lips when I told her to make the coffee *strong*.

And I'm thinking about how those lips might look wrapped around the head of my thick cock, sliding down my shaft. *Fuck*, it's a good mental image, one that gets me hard as a rock sitting here at the breakfast table.

"Jesus," Kieran says, waving one hand in front of my face. "Hey, your royal goddamn highness."

I snap out of it.

"What?"

"If you want to head over Friday, we're taking the private jet straight from here," he says. "Otherwise, you can find your *own* goddamn private jet."

"I *have* got one," I point out. "Two, if you count the little jet."

"Yeah, but ours will be way more fun," Beckett says, grinning through his hangover. "Our staff has been interviewing stewardesses for days."

The application list for the position of *stewardess on Prince Beckett's Private Plane* is a mile long — and when the rumors about Beckett and Kieran got out, the list only got longer.

They're both notorious playboys in their own right, but their absolute favorite thing to do? Share a woman. The thought's never done it for me, so I've never tried it, but the two of them would fuck the same woman all day long if they could.

"Are you taking requests?" Declan asks.

"Let me guess," Beckett says. "Blonde, long legs, make a good champagne cocktail, and doesn't have a gag reflex."

We all laugh.

"You forgot the most important part," Declan says. "Must like big dicks."

Across the restaurant, the waitress comes out of the kitchen and walks across the room to another table, two old ladies who just sat down. Instantly, the guys' chatter turns to noise as I watch her hand them menus and take their order.

She's *not* my type. My type is barely-there skirts and low-cut dresses, women who lick their lips when they look at me and who whisper things like *is everything I've heard about His Royal Hardness true?*

My type is women gasping with delight when they find out that the rumors *are* true, then invite their friends over so they can all take turns riding my massive pole.

Not sweet, beautiful breakfast waitresses.

Or at least, not yet, because I'm changing my mind pretty damn fast. There's something about the curve of her neck, the swell of her breasts, the way she cocks her hips when she stands that's making me achingly hard, even though she's just wearing a t-shirt and shorts.

"Just fuck her," Kieran says, his voice cutting through thoughts of my cock pressed between her perky breasts, her eyes half-closed with desire.

"Seriously," Declan agrees. "Go bang her in the men's room and then come back so we can have a goddamn *conversation*."

My eyes caress the curve of her ass one more time, and then they return to the table.

"Because you're a *scintillating* conversationalist when you're hungover as fuck yourself," I say.

Declan just rolls his eyes.

"Suit yourself," he says.

I look over at her again as she takes the old ladies' menus, smiles, and turns back toward the kitchen, still stiff as fuck in the tuxedo pants I've been wearing for twelve hours. Not that it's going to matter. I've bent women over bathroom sinks and fucked them so hard they forgot their own names wearing way worse than this, and I can probably do it again now.

No problem. Give me two minutes and I bet I can have this sweet, innocent girl *screaming* my name.

Chapter Three

Ella

He's looking at me again.

Not looking. That's not the right word. He's practically groping me with his eyes, running them down my body, and he's not shy about it.

I almost drop the coffee pot as I walk toward their table.

It's not that I never get lecherous looks. Plenty of dirty old men come in here, and I catch them staring at me all the time. It stopped bothering me a long time ago.

But he's not a dirty old man. He's hot as sin, muscled and cocky and clearly used to getting what he wants. He's disheveled in exactly the right way, in a way that makes me want to let him dishevel *me*.

Not that I know much about getting disheveled. I'm a virgin, after all — I've never gotten further than some experimental kisses with a boy back in high school.

Right now, I wish I was thinking about *anything* but straddling his lap, sliding my hips against his. Putting my hands underneath his half-unbuttoned shirt as he groans, taking my breasts in both hands...

"Doesn't look half bad," that rough, gritty voice says as I pour coffee into *his* mug.

"You did say strong," I say, as sweetly as I can muster.

"Think you got it right?" he asks, smirking.

What an asshole.

"I'm sure you'll tell me if I didn't," I say, still smiling as I pour the other three men coffee. They're all good-looking despite their hangovers, but none of them makes my breath catch in my throat quite the way *he* does.

The jerk. Of course.

Just get them breakfast and be done with it, Ella.

He takes a sip as I place the carafe on the table. There's something sensual about even *that*, the way his lips move, the way his eyes linger on mine.

"It needs sugar," he finally says. "Got any?"

I point at the sugar container on the table, in plain sight. He looks at it, then takes another sip.

"Got any other sugar?" he asks, his eyes raking down my body. His three friends all smirk, and I feel my face heating up again.

"We've got Sweet & Low, Equal, stevia, and I think there's some—"

He just laughs.

"Nevermind," he says. "I'll have the pancakes."

They all order, and I practically sprint back to the kitchen. We're finally getting busy with the breakfast rush, so Flynn's just cooking, flipping things, and shouting questions at me. Thank God he doesn't notice that I'm red-faced and flustered, because I'm absolutely positive there would be questions about it.

He was hitting on me, right? Asking me for sugar? It's not the first time I've been asked that, in *that* way, but it's the first time I've kind of considered it.

Not that I was really considering it. What exactly am I supposed to do, follow him into the men's room and let him bend me over the sink? Let him pull my hair as he pushes my shorts down, sliding his fingers through my dripping wet—

"Excuse me, miss," one of the old ladies calls, and I realize I was just staring at the wall, my panties slowing soaking through thinking about the things this total stranger could do to me in the bathroom.

"Could we please get the check?"

"Of course!" I chirp, and grab it out of my apron.

When the food comes up for the jerk's table, I pretend I'm busy with my three other tables and beg the other waitress, Chloe, to give it to them.

She comes back wide-eyed.

"Jerks, right?" I whisper, checking an order against the ticket.

Chloe grabs me by the shoulder and turns me around.

"You could have told me that *Prince Grayson* was here," she hisses.

I'm stunned. My mouth drops open.

"What?" I squeak out.

Chloe just makes an *are you kidding me right now* face, and Flynn comes over.

"Did you just say Prince Grayson is here?" he asks, spatula still in hand.

Chloe nods wordlessly.

"You gave them menus!" I whisper at Flynn. "You didn't know either!"

"It was dark! They weren't looking at me! I was in a hurry because *your* ass was late, girl!" he says, rolling his eyes. "Besides, Prince Grayson is one hot-ass hunk of man, and those boys over there are hungover wrecks."

I disagree, having already thought several times this morning about that hungover wreck between my thighs, but I don't say anything.

"Do we give them a discount?" Chloe whispers.

"Hell no!" Flynn says, darting his eyes at the table. "He's richer than God, he doesn't get a *discount*."

"What do we do?" I whisper.

We all look at each other. Chloe and Flynn shrug.

"Make sure they get lots of refills?" she says. Flynn nods in agreement.

For the rest of the time they're there, I'm super awkward. I don't know if they're here because they don't want to be recognized, so I don't say anything, but I know I'm acting weird and *not* just because looking at the guy makes me wet as a waterfall.

Instead of asking for the check, Prince Grayson just hands me an all-black credit card. I'm almost nervous to run it through our machine, because just this card looks like something way too fancy for me to touch.

When they're finally leaving, I heave a sigh of relief. I just want to have a regular morning at work, not a morning where all I can think about is the incredibly sexy crown prince and the *things* I want him to do to me. Even though he's a jerk.

I'm wiping down a table when I turn around, and he's right behind me, that stupid smirk on his handsome face, that cocky look in his eyes. My breath catches in my throat, and I don't say anything, just stand there like an idiot.

"What do you say to taking a well-deserved break?" he says, his voice low and growly. "You've been on

13

your feet all morning, might be nice to be on your knees for a few minutes."

I open my mouth, then shut it, turning bright red.

"I'd return the favor, naturally," he says, still smirking. "Ever wondered why they call me *His Royal Hardness?* The rumors are true. Think of how you could brag to your friends."

I look down. I can't help it. I try not to read the tabloids, because *ew*, but everyone in the kingdom knows that Prince Grayson is legendarily well-endowed. Hell, he got photographed drunk and naked a few months ago, and Flynn waxed rhapsodical about his magnificent cock.

I didn't look at the pictures. It felt wrong and weird, but right now I'm staring at the enormous bulge in his tuxedo pants, and even though I'm not exactly an expert on penises — okay, fine, I've never seen one in person — it seems like they can't possibly be that big.

"What do you say?" he asks, putting one hand on the table behind me and leaning in. "Fancy a quick fuck before you get back to work?"

I duck to one side, heart hammering because I can't *believe* he's propositioning me like this. I'm a nice girl, a virgin, not some coked-up partier who'd say yes to *having sex in the bathroom while I'm at work*.

No matter *how* sexy this guy is. Even though he's the Prince. I'm not swiping my v-card like this.

"No!" I manage to squeak out.

He just laughs.

"You just mean not here," he says, still cocky as ever. "How about I pay off your boss for the rest of your shift, call my limousine, and you can find out what it feels like to come for royalty?"

I'm the color of a tomato, I just know it. My face is hotter than a furnace, my heart thumping in my chest.

"I have tables!" I say, then finally manage to duck around him.

I practically *run* into the kitchen, and I don't come out until I'm completely certain he's gone.

Chapter Four

Grayson

Declan, Beckett, and Kieran give me shit the whole way home because I couldn't close the deal with some commoner breakfast waitress, and I roll my eyes and try to play it off. It's not like I've never been turned down before. No one gets lucky every single time, but it's sure an unusual feeling.

After all, girls flock to *me*. I haven't chased anyone in years, because there's simply no need. I've never met a girl worth going after like that, not when there are literally thousands of women who'd get on their knees for me in a heartbeat.

It's nearing nine in the morning when we finally pull through the gates of the castle. The other three are staying here on an extended vacation — it's a castle, so we've got the room, after all, and we stumble out of our limousine and through the garage door, getting looks from some of the household staff.

They're carefully neutral looks, of course. The household staff aren't idiots. They know better than to let what they're thinking show on their faces, but I'm not stupid.

They're thinking *I can't believe he's getting home at nine in the morning again when I started dusting chandeliers at eight.*

Well, some are thinking that. I've dallied with more than a few of the younger female members — all right, and some of the older ones because I like a cougar now and then — and *they're* all wondering when I'll ask them to my chambers again.

Beckett slaps me on the shoulder as he heads off to his guest bedroom, and Declan gives me a friendly shoulder-punch.

"Better luck next time, mate," he says. "Maybe tonight we'll go out and take the edge off, yeah?"

I know *take the edge off* means *find another girl to fuck,* and I grin in agreement.

"Sounds perfect," I say, and we walk in separate directions.

My bedroom is more like a wing of the castle, a suite of a dozen rooms. Hell, I've got a conference room, a kitchen, a living room, three bathrooms and my own patio.

I toss my tuxedo into the dry-cleaning hamper and walk to the bathroom totally naked. If there's one thing I've learned, going straight to bed after an all-night bender is just about the worst thing you can do.

Prince Grayson's number one rule of living the high life? Take a shower after a night out, before you get in bed. You'll thank yourself later.

My bathroom's got its own jacuzzi, marble countertops, mirrors everywhere, the whole nine yards. It's fucking fancy, but I just want to get clean so I hop into the standing shower, turn it onto hot, and lather up.

The second I close my eyes under the stream of water, I see *her*. The hot waitress, just slightly bending over our table, her shorts tight against her luscious ass for a split second.

And blood just fucking *rushes* to His Royal Hardness. I wish I knew what it was about that girl, but I've got no clue whatsoever. I just know that thinking about her makes me hard as fuck like no other girl has in a long, long time.

Maybe ever.

I wrap one fist around my cock, the hot water still hitting me full in the chest, and start stroking myself slowly. I try to imagine the girl from two nights ago whose name I either didn't know or forgot: tiny, short, low-cut dress. No bra, fake breasts, nipples hard as rocks as she straddled me in the VIP section of the club we were in, not caring at all that virtually everyone could see her tiny thong as her skirt rode up.

But then I think about the waitress. Her pink lips, slightly open in surprise. The way she'd *look* at me if I unbuttoned the top of her uniform, maybe the way her eyelids would flutter as I kissed her neck...

I squeeze my eyes shut, grit my teeth, and command myself to think about the brunette. The way she was on her knees before the bathroom door even closed, the way she gasped with delight when she unzipped my pants and freed my monster cock, the way she inhaled me while looking up through her thick eyelashes.

And then she's the waitress, and she's not in the bathroom but she's in my bedroom. She's got one hand wrapped around the base of my cock as she licks the swollen head slowly, then puts her lips around it, sucking and licking. I put my hand on her head and push her down, slowly, until I hit the back of her mouth and groan out loud, the noise echoing through the shower.

I give up on trying to imagine the other girl. I'm too far gone thinking about the waitress, her lips around my cock as she sucks me harder and harder, her eyes *begging* me to use her, take her, claim her —

I come with a grunt, one hand against the shower wall, and I keep stroking until I'm totally spent and suddenly exhausted as all hell. I can tell that little jerk-off session isn't gonna do it where the waitress is concerned, but it was better than nothing.

I rinse off one last time, get out of the shower, dry off, and fall into bed. I gotta have the energy to go back out tonight and *really* forget this girl, after all.

· · ·

I haven't been asleep for nearly long enough when there's a loud banging on my door. I get up, not bothering to put on more than the boxer-briefs I'm wearing, and open the door to my suite.

It's George, my father's valet, and probably the person he trusts the most in the world. George doesn't bat an eye at my state of undress, but if he's here in person, I know I'm about to be in big fucking trouble from the other person in the kingdom who can actually create problems for me.

My father, of course. The King.

"Your father wishes a word with you, Your Highness," George says. His face stays impressively neutral, though it's not as if he hasn't seen me in a far worse state before.

I run one hand through my hair.

"Right now?" I ask. The clock says it's about four

in the afternoon.

"Yes. He didn't seem to think that you'd be indisposed," George says.

What he means is *you shouldn't be asleep, it's four in the fucking afternoon*, but George would never *ever* use that sort of language.

But this might be bad. My father rarely wants to see me, and he *never* sends George to wake me up. I run my hand through my hair again, wondering if I can get out of this, but I think I'm stuck.

"Let me get decent," I mutter.

"Of course," George says, ever polite.

Fuck. This might be bad. *Fuck.*

Chapter Five

Ella

"You're kidding me," Flynn says, scraping off the griddle.

I'm standing on the other side of the service window, rolling napkins around silverware for tomorrow morning.

"He really hit on me that way," I say, and shrug. "The man is famous for not being able to keep it in his pants, Flynn, I think I was just the closest available person with breasts and two legs."

I don't tell Flynn that for the rest of my shift, I couldn't think about *anything* else. I didn't really consider taking the prince up on his offer — if nothing else, my stepmother would find out and she'd probably lock me in the basement for a month — but all day I've been fantasizing about the enormous bulge in his pants.

I've been thinking about the prince, in his

limousine, bending me over the back seat and sliding the head of that *monster* along my lips, one hand in my hair, holding me down. Making me absolutely delirious with anticipation before he finally pushed it inside me—

"Earth to Ella," Flynn says again, waving a spatula in my direction.

"Huh?"

"I *said*, give yourself a little more credit, girl. And I said it about twenty times. Daydreaming?"

I blush. I've always hated that about myself — I blush way too easily.

"No!"

He grins.

"You *sure*?"

"Of course I'm sure."

"Prince Grayson's a sexy-ass fox, girl. I'd let him fuck me in the men's bathroom for *sure*," he says, reaching for a rag. "Thomas would understand. Thomas would probably want to watch."

Flynn winks at me, and I just blush harder. He laughs, because he loves getting a rise out of me.

"Well, it's not like I'm ever going to see him again," I point out. "And I wouldn't see him again even if I had, you know, gone into the bathroom with him, so it's for the best."

Flynn just sighs dramatically, and I glance at the clock. It's four-thirty.

Crap. I drop the silverware I'm holding back into its trays, and Flynn glances over.

"I gotta go," I say. "You're good here, right?"

He waves the rag at me.

"Which troll-beast needs you to pluck her nose hairs again because she can't figure out which end of the tweezers to use?" he asks.

"*Shhh*," I hiss, shooting him a glare. "Come on, don't get me in trouble."

"Everyone else is gone, you know," he says.

"I've gotta make dinner, then make sure Peyton's gown is pressed and ready," I say. "She's going to the opera tonight with some rich duke, I forget which one."

"For her sake, I hope he's blind," Flynn says.

"Flynn!"

He just laughs.

"Go on, get," he says, and I rush out the door.

• • •

I'm barely in the front door when the screeching starts, echoing down the wide foyer of my father's mansion.

My *deceased* father's mansion. Technically, that makes it my stepmother's, since she inherited everything because he didn't leave a will, but I still think of it as his.

There's not a lot of his that I have left, so it helps.

"Ella! *Where* is my flat iron? The ceramic one? Did you borrow it again? I swear to God my hair is an absolute nightmare!"

Peyton's voice feels like an icepick to my eardrums, and I take a deep breath while I close the front door, trying to collect myself.

For the record, I've never borrowed her flat iron. My hair is naturally straight to begin with, and besides, I'm not insane. She'd probably skin me alive if I even asked.

"ELLA!!"

"I think I saw it in the middle drawer of your bathroom counter when I was cleaning in there last week," I call.

There's no answer, just angry footsteps stomping around upstairs. She doesn't shout for me again, so I assume she's found the stupid flat iron and I can get on with my day.

As quickly as I can, I head to my own room, a small one attached to the laundry room, change out of my uniform and into regular clothes. I pull my hair back into a bun again, then head into the kitchen so I can make dinner.

Slade is outside, sunning herself by the pool in a bikini that doesn't really flatter her figure, but she likes to think it does. When she sees me through the window, she waves at me, then crooks her finger.

My blood boils, but I go see what she wants.

"I need a margarita," she says. She's wearing sunglasses, but I'm pretty sure she doesn't even open her eyes again.

I'm tempted to say *then go make yourself a margarita*, but I don't. She'll tell her mother, and then I'd be in big trouble.

"Sure," I say, and head back into the kitchen. There's a pitcher of margarita mix in the fridge, and I mix Slade up a strong one — the sooner she gets drunk, the sooner she'll fall asleep and leave me alone. She could easily do this herself, but why do anything yourself when your stepsister is practically your indentured servant?

Finally, when both my stepsisters are happy, I can start making dinner. Tonight's menu is hazelnut-crusted lamb chops, which my stepmother specifically requested even though I know for a fact she doesn't like hazelnuts. She'll just try it, push it away, and demand something else.

Still, even though I'm busy, as the nuts whirl in the

food processor my mind slips to Prince Grayson one more time, and I close my eyes, imagining him behind me right now. His lips on the back of my neck, his hand in my hair.

The way he'd bend me over this counter, squeeze my butt. The sound of his zipper sliding down.

"Are you finally making dinner?" Livia's voice says, sharp even over the din of the food processor, and my eyes snap open.

"Yes," I say.

She looks me over, sharp gray eyes in a pinched face, bottle-blonde hair waved to hair-sprayed perfection. For one second I wonder if she somehow *knows* what I was just thinking about, but then she walks on.

"Good," she calls over her shoulder. "Peyton's got a big date with a very important man, and she doesn't want to miss it."

She leaves the room, and I allow myself a tiny smile.

Not as important as the man who propositioned me this morning, I think.

Sometimes it's the small victories.

Chapter Six

Grayson

"What the hell is *this?*" my father roars, slapping a tabloid onto his enormous mahogany desk.

I lean in, just enough to read the headline.

"I'M PREGNANT WITH PRINCE GRAYSON'S BABY!"

It's in screamingly bright yellow print over a picture of me and some girl, dancing in a nightclub. Or, rather, she's dancing — bent in half at the waist, ass up — and I'm standing there with a drink.

"Who the hell is this—" he checks the magazine again, "—this Dakota Williamson?"

I squint at the picture, desperately trying to place it. Despite the headline, I sincerely doubt that she's pregnant with my child. I may get my dick wet a lot, but I'm careful. I know perfectly well that half the women in the kingdom would *love* to bear my child for the support payments alone.

Call me old-fashioned, but I'd prefer not to have twenty different baby mamas.

"I'm not sure," I say truthfully, and my father just *glares*.

"I'll tell you who she is," he says, his voice rising even more. "She's some strumpet who's the daughter of an *equally* useless brown-nosing earl who's been a pain in my ass for years."

I look at the picture again, and *finally* that night clicks.

Dakota gave *great* head, but I didn't fuck her. There's *definitely* no way she's pregnant by me.

"She's lying," I say, and tell my father why, though I leave the details vague. It doesn't seem to make him less angry, though, and he launches himself to his feet.

King Maxwell is still an intimidating man. Even though we're the same height, same build, and I'm thirty years younger, he's still got that aura of authority and power that comes with being king.

"I've had enough," he proclaims, pacing back and forth on the expensive rug.

I don't answer. I don't think I'm supposed to, really.

"It's time you settled down, Grayson."

The sentence hits me like a punch in the face. Settle down? Is he kidding?

The longest relationship I've ever had lasted two weeks, and that was only because the girl and I didn't speak the same language. It was purely, *purely* physical, though I do still know how to say *fuck me deeper* in Russian.

But I got bored of Svetlana. It's what I do, I get bored of girls and want to move on to the next one.

"Father, I—"

"It's not up for discussion," he says, turning sharply in his tracks and glaring at me. "I've had it with your behavior, Grayson. At first, when you were more discreet, I could handle it. But now, like *this*—"

He gestures furiously at the tabloid.

"This is a drain on the kingdom, the royal family, *everything*. And I won't have it."

I jump to my feet, fists balled at my side.

"You can't just *decree* that," I say.

He stops and just *looks* at me.

"Yes, I can," he says coolly. "Just like I can decree that if you don't stop bringing shame on our family and nation, you can be disinherited and your sister Aurora can become queen someday."

He wouldn't. He fucking *wouldn't*.

But the look in my father's eyes is telling me he's not kidding. He might really do this, because as my father, he's the only person I know more strong-willed and bull-headed than I am.

"We'll do this the old-fashioned way," he says when I don't respond. "What do you say to a proper ball. We'll invite every eligible woman in the kingdom, and you can pick your bride from there."

The kingdom is very small, because otherwise there's no way that would work.

"I'm supposed to choose after one night?" I ask, a sarcastic undertone creeping into my voice.

"No," my father says, unperturbed. "You're supposed to narrow down the pool of possible candidates after one night. I'm well aware that we're no longer living in medieval times."

Out of nowhere, I think about the waitress. I don't know a thing about her — she wasn't even wearing a name tag — but if she's eligible, she'll be there.

Fuck it. I'll *decree* that all women have to come, just to make sure she's there.

I still hate this plan. I don't want to settle down with the waitress, I just want to fuck her once, make her *writhe* with the kind of pleasure that I'm somehow certain no one's ever shown her before.

I want to see her pretty pink lips around my cock, those blue eyes looking up at my shyly while she takes me in her mouth, her blonde hair wrapped around my hand.

"All right," I say, and for once my father looks surprised, like he was expecting a fight.

"Excellent," he says, though he sounds suspicious. "We'll set a date. The sooner the better. How about one week from tonight?"

An image flashes through my brain: the waitress in an evening gown, low-cut and low-backed, hugging all her curves. A week can't go fast enough.

"One week sounds good, Father," I say.

He levels one finger at me.

"If a tabloid so much as *prints your name* between now and then, I'll—"

I hold both my hands up, palms out.

"They won't," I say, even as annoyance twists inside me.

The World Cup this weekend is *definitely* out. Goodbye beautiful Italian girls, goodbye eager stewardesses sucking my cock. Goodbye watching one girl ride me hard while her friend plays with her nipples from behind.

But strangely, I don't feel *that* bad. I'm not sure I'll miss it all that much, and I'm not sure why.

"I'll have George start making the arrangements," my father says. "And thank you for being so reasonable, son."

I duck my head once, unsure what to say. My father rarely thanks me for anything.

"My pleasure," I say, and then I leave his office.

Chapter Seven

Ella

Peyton is a nightmare. She doesn't want to eat the dinner I made because she says walnuts make her bloated, and then she blames me because she can't get the zipper of the evening gown she wants to wear all the way up.

"Try *harder*," she demands, looking at herself in a full-length mirror.

She's fully done up, hair piled on her head, fake eyelashes, ruby-red lips. The gown she chose is a shimmery blue.

Peyton's not an ugly girl. She's actually kind of pretty — at least she is before she insists on spackling makeup onto her face with a trowel and wearing a dress that's a size too small for her. Every time she goes on a date I'm tempted to remind her that no one's going to be looking at the number on her tag, but I never have.

"Try holding your breath," I suggest.

"I *am*," she insists.

I tug. The zipper's not going up, and I'm worried that I'm going to break it.

"Is there another dress you could wear?" I ask. I know she's got a closet full of them, but I also know that's not necessarily good enough for her.

"The Duke likes blue," she insists. "And I like how this one makes my cleavage look good."

I sigh silently, to myself, looking over Peyton's shoulder at my own reflection. I look tired and bedraggled. I just want her to go on her stupid date so I can go do the dishes and then read in my tiny room while no one bothers me.

But instead I hear Livia coming up the stairs.

"Peyton!" she shouts, the sound like nails on a chalkboard. "Are you ready yet?"

"Ella can't zip up my dress!"

I suppress the urge to roll my eyes at Peyton acting like this is *my* fault as Livia storms into the room and gives Peyton a once-over.

"Either put on a corset or change your dress," she commands.

Peyton pouts, but she doesn't disobey her mother. She tosses the blue dress into a heap on the floor and grabs an aquamarine one from the closet. This one zips up perfectly.

I breathe a quiet sigh of relief.

After that, there's drama about Peyton's shoes and drama about Peyton's purse, but then the Duke's limousine finally pulls up and she leaves. Slade's had a couple of margaritas and she's watching TV in her own quarters, and Livia's probably got souls to steal somewhere, so I'm finally left alone.

I do the dishes. I clean the kitchen, the dining room,

and pick up after the three of them in the downstairs of the giant mansion. It's work, but I do this every night — by now, the rhythm is kind of soothing, to be honest.

After all that, I head to my bedroom. It's a smallish room in what was once the servants' quarters, which isn't lost on me, but since it's so plain and simple, my stepfamily almost never comes this way. And it's not like I live in squalor — my room is on the small side, but well-kept, with a bed, a dresser, a comfy chair, and a window that looks east that I can watch the sunrise from.

Right now, there's a family of hummingbirds who've made their home in a bush right outside the window, with three tiny eggs waiting to hatch, though I can't see them right now since it's dark.

I pull the curtains, take off my shoes, grab my book, and finally flop into the comfortable chair. It was deemed too out-of-fashion for the living room several years ago, but I still like it. I curl up, turn on the light, and start reading.

I get about two paragraphs in before I'm distracted again, thinking about the prince. I keep thinking about him, whether I'm cooking or doing the dishes or helping Peyton get ready, and it's... uncomfortable.

I've never felt this way before, not in the least. I mean, I've had crushes but I've never wanted anyone to do the things that I can't help thinking about now.

Stop it and read your book, I order myself. I get through one more paragraph.

Then I realize I'm thinking about Prince Grayson's hand slowly making its way up my thigh, under the skirt of my diner uniform, and I bite my lip. In my fantasy, he's got me up against the table, my hips pressed into the formica, and he's grabbing my hair with his other hand, pulling my head back *just* hard enough.

I swallow, the words on the page swimming in front of me.

There's something thick and massive against my ass, and a jolt of heat shoots straight through my core at the thought, my entrance suddenly wet as fantasy-Grayson shoves his hand all the way up my skirt, still pushing me against the table, and strokes me through my panties.

I gasp, and realize my eyes are shut. I open them just as my book falls from my hands, forgotten, and I just look at it on the floor.

Then I unbutton the jeans I'm wearing and slide one hand underneath them, beneath my panties. I'm slick and wet, and when I find my sensitive nub I sigh with relief, rubbing it quickly beneath my fingers.

I think about Grayson, doing the same. About him shoving my skirt over my hips. Smacking my ass and laughing in my ear. Pinching my nipples and making me moan.

My finger moves faster as I bite my lip, forcing myself not to make any noise, but I need *more*. This isn't enough.

I move my hand lower and slide two fingers inside myself, moving them gently in my tightness, feeling myself clench and flutter at the delicious thoughts I'm having.

I think about him shoving my panties down, the sound of his zipper, the feel of his cock as it rubs along my ass, one hand still in my hair. I move my fingers inside myself harder, faster, biting my lip as I imagine Prince Grayson's cock at my entrance.

And then I fuck myself even harder, biting my lip, and my back arches and my toes curl as I finish *hard* to the thought of him sinking his huge cock inside me to the hilt and the way he'd groan as he did.

I've never fantasized like this before, never wanted a man to bend me over and fuck me like that. I slowly pull my fingers out and my pants back up, buttoning them with trembling hands.

What's gotten into me? I wonder.

And then immediately, I think: *I guess I know what I want to get into me.*

Just the thought makes me blush stop-sign red, and I practically run to go wash my hands.

Chapter Eight

Grayson

"I don't *know* her name," I explain for at least the tenth time. "She works at the Tremaine Diner, over on Fourth and Saint Fleury Boulevard. She's blonde, blue-eyed..."

I trail off, because the three women opposite me at this table have just gone silent.

"So you have no name, no address, no phone number, no nickname..." the first one says. She's very no-nonsense, with short brown hair and big brown eyes.

"No," I admit.

"And even though we've found pictures of everyone who's listed as working at this diner, she's not among them," the second woman says, a slightly chubby girl with crazy red hair and a button nose.

"How sure are you that she exists?" asks their boss. She's in her fifties, outfitted in an elegant business suit, and wears her gray hair like a helmet. The kind of woman that simply seems *incredibly* competent.

"I'm not crazy," I say. "Try checking the employees who have quit recently, or just started? How up-to-date were the records you looked through?"

"Very," says Competence Herself.

"You're sure it was *that* diner?" says redhead.

I bury my head in my hands.

"Check all the diners," I say. "Just fucking find this girl, okay?"

I glance up. They're looking at each other.

"I'll compile a list of all the diners in a half-mile radius," No-Nonsense Brunette says.

"No, *all* the diners," I insist. "I'm not insane. She was there, I saw her. Maybe it was a different diner, but *this girl needs to be at the ball.*"

They all stare at me in silence, and I realize that with the last sentence, I just slammed my hand onto the table in front of myself. I lift it up silently, then stand.

"Thank you," I say, then walk out of the room.

• • •

I don't know what's happening. Planning this ball has taken up most of the past couple days — I think George nearly died when my father told him he needed to organize an enormous ball within a week — but all I can think about is the waitress.

I've gone back to the diner every day. Fuck, I've gone to half the diners in the city, because I was half-drunk and half-hungover and I'm not even sure I remember which one it was.

And I haven't found her again. Even though my memory of this girl is crystal clear enough for me to jerk off to twice a day, I'm starting to think that maybe

I *am* crazy. Maybe the event planners I was just talking to are right, and I just made this girl up in a drug and alcohol-fueled haze.

As I'm walking down a palace hallway, my phone buzzes. It's Declan, asking if I want to go out with them tonight since I had to miss the World Cup.

I think about it for a moment.

This is exactly what you need, I think. *Go out, get laid — get laid twice — and get your mind off this waitress who might not even exist.*

Just play it low-key and don't get into trouble with your father.

I text back *Hell yes!* and he texts me a champagne bottle emoji, and suddenly I'm relieved to be doing something.

Besides, they're not gonna believe what happened while they were in Florence.

• • •

"You are *fucking* kidding me," Beckett says.

"I wish," I say, taking a long drink from my champagne glass.

"Settle down meaning *get married?*" Kieran says, his face simply astonished.

The four of us are in the back of the Sapphire Spot nightclub. On the dance floor, lights are flashing and the beat is thumping, scantily-dressed people gyrating everywhere.

I *should* be having a great time, but I'm not really. I try to make myself watch a girl on the dance floor shake her ass and lean over, practically showing everyone her tits, but it doesn't even hold my interest.

"Yup," I confirm, leaning back in the booth. "That's what he meant. Get hitched or get disinherited, my choice."

Declan just shakes his head.

"You know what that means, right?" he says.

I shrug.

"You gotta go out with a bang," he grins.

I force myself to grin back, even though I don't really feel like it right now.

"That's exactly the point," I say, and the rest of them laugh so I *must* sound sincere. "Just don't get me busted, guys. If I show up in the papers again I'm toast."

Twenty minutes later, our booth is practically *flooded* with girls. Declan's got one on his lap and one next to him, and they're alternating between making out with each other and making out with him.

There's three over by Beckett and Kieran, and though they're all giggling and laughing, each of them has his hand on the same girl's ass. I think I know which one they're sharing *tonight*.

And me? There's a redhead on my lap, though her hair is almost definitely fake, and she's squirming around like a snake or something. Her tits are fake, and I can see her nipples through the shimmery pink material. After all, she's practically shoving them up my nose.

"I've heard you've got a nickname," she says in a baby-sweet voice, one finger on my chest. Like she's suddenly coy or something.

I slide my hand over her ass, and even though it's a nice ass, my cock doesn't even twitch.

"And what's that?" I say, my response practiced after hearing this a thousand times.

She smiles and leans in, her lips close to my ear.

"His Royal Hardness," she purrs.

Too bad right now His Royal Hardness is limper

than a wet spaghetti noodle.

"Do they," I say, the words on autopilot. "Why do they say that?"

Her finger makes its way slowly down my chest, her lips still close to my ear. I close my eyes because of the sudden unpleasant prickling making its way down my spine.

"Because I've heard you have a king-sized cock and you know how to use it," she whispers, her hand now on my lower belly.

A wave of revulsion passes through me, and suddenly I need to leave, *now*. I need her to get off me and I need to go outside and be somewhere, *anywhere* else.

I take a deep breath. I've never tried to get myself *out* of this situation before, so I'm not quite sure how to do it.

"Would you mind getting up for a moment?" I ask, politely as I can.

She pouts, not getting up, so I turn on the charm and grin at her as wickedly as I can.

"If you're going to be a naughty girl, I'll have to punish you when I get back," I say, lowering my voice until it's a growl while I palm her ass, then squeeze. "And you *know* how I punish naughty girls."

"Do you promise?" she purrs, fluttering her eyelashes.

"I'm not going to dignify that with an answer," I say, blatantly staring at her tits.

It works. She stands, wobbling slightly in her sky-high heels.

"I'll be right back," I say, and leave. I don't even say goodbye to the other guys — they've all got their faces buried in their respective women, and they'll figure out that I've left eventually.

I head toward the men's room, but instead of heading in I push open an exit door into an alleyway, and as it clicks behind me, I take a deep breath of the clear, cool night air.

I don't know what's happening to me. I've never *done* that before, turned down a hot, ready-to-go girl, but I suddenly just had to get out of there.

Unbidden, I think about the waitress, yet-a-fucking-gain. How if *she* were wriggling like that on my lap I'd already be balls deep inside her, watching her face as her eyes rolled back as she felt every inch of me.

And fuck, *there's* His Royal Hardness. Goddamn it, why couldn't that happen a minute ago with the redhead?

I consider going back in and seeing if I can keep it up for her, but I'm just not in the mood. Instead I call my driver to pick me up, then head home early.

At least I won't be in any goddamn tabloids.

Chapter Nine

Ella

When I get home the next day, Peyton and Slade are gathered around the dining room table squealing. Literally squealing, the sound so high-pitched it's kind of hard to take.

Maybe there's a new line of luxury eyeshadow, I think as I walk toward them.

"It's so *fancy*," Peyton breathes.

"It's calligraphied and embossed," Slade says authoritatively, as if she knows anything about either of those.

"Do you think he wrote it himself?" Peyton asks.

"He has such *sexy* handwriting."

"Oh my god, what if he licked the envelope?"

I edge closer, wondering what they could possibly be talking about.

"What should we *wear*?"

"Oh my God."

"Oh. My *God*."

I walk into the room, and they both turn toward me, their mouths partly open, each holding a thick square of paper in her hand.

"Ella," Slade says, her voice as serious as I've ever heard it. "We have a really big week ahead of us."

I don't respond, just raise my eyebrows.

"The prince. Is throwing. A ball," Peyton adds, then holds out her piece of paper to me.

It's an invitation.

YOUR PRESENCE IS REQUESTED
At the Royal Palace, Crystal Ballroom
Friday, May 17
Eight in the Evening

All eligible young women are strongly requested to attend.
Black tie.

I just read the invitation and don't say anything for a long moment. It's not like I know Prince Grayson even a little — we interacted for about five minutes total, and my extensive fantasies about him since don't count — but he didn't exactly seem like the formal ball type.

"Why do you think all eligible women are supposed to attend?" Peyton asks.

I hand the invitation back, keeping my mouth shut. Slade gasps.

"Maybe he's looking for a wife," she says, her eyes going wide. "That's why he sleeps around so much. He's just been searching for the right woman this whole time, and now he's almost given up finding her. This is his one last chance..."

She stares off into the distance, lost in her romantic

reverie, and I leave and head to the kitchen before I laugh so hard I snort. Not that I know Prince Grayson beyond being shamelessly hit on, but I've got a feeling that he hasn't been searching for his soulmate this entire time.

I'm pretty sure he's just searching for his next conquest.

I make dinner, we eat, and then I clean the kitchen and do the dishes. Peyton and Slade don't talk about *anything* but the ball, and their mother Livia actually encourages them.

They're all being stupid. Whatever reason the prince is throwing this ball for, with such short notice, it's not so he can find a wife. It's not the fifteen hundreds any more, and that's not how people date these days. It's probably to announce his engagement to some high-born noblewoman or a princess from another country, and when Peyton and Slade realize what they're there for, they'll be crushed.

I almost feel bad for them. *Almost.*

But I keep thinking about the ball, like I've been thinking about Grayson almost non-stop. I don't know what's gotten into me, but I've replayed our interaction in my head at least a hundred times. I've thought endlessly about what could have happened if I'd said yes instead of no.

And weirdest of all? I think I'm beginning to regret my answer.

Not that I wanted to swipe my v-card in the bathroom at work or in the back of a limousine, but maybe if I had, I could stop thinking about it so much. Besides, everyone loses their virginity at some point, or almost everyone — why not get a good story out of it?

By the time I've done my chores and turned in for the night, I've decided.

I'm an eligible woman.

I'm going to ask Livia if I can go to the ball.

• • •

Livia purses her lips. The shape looks vaguely sea-creature like, thanks to extensive fillers and plastic surgery.

"You want to go to the ball," she says, tapping a finger against one cheek."

"I'm an eligible woman," I say quietly.

"Well, technically, that's a little bit up in the air, isn't it?" she says, her gaze as cold as steel.

My stomach hardens into a knot, because she's right.

Technically, even though I'm twenty-two, Livia is still my legal guardian and custodian. Any money that I have, she controls. If I run away, the cops deliver me back here.

I found out the hard way a long time ago that it's better to just stay.

"My debt is nearly paid," I point out.

She leans back in her chair, an off-white baroque monstrosity that she's *so* proud of.

"Are you remembering to count interest?" she asks, her tone of voice not changing.

Instantly, my blood boils. The interest is new. She mentioned it for the first time last year when I pointed out that I was nearly paid off, and that was the first time I realized that I have no power in this situation. None.

After my father died, Livia paid for my room, board, and education. She paid for it from my dead father's money, but she resented having to spend money on me at all, so she devised a scheme.

Livia decided that I *owed* her for all that. Tens of thousands of dollars.

And Livia's got friends. Powerful, influential friends, and they're the ones who granted her custodianship over me, even though I'm legally an adult.

I'm trapped here until I've worked my debt off, and when Livia decided that interest was included, my term got a whole lot longer.

"Yes, I'm counting the interest," I whisper.

"You know that even if he's looking to marry, he's not looking for you," she says, her voice still cool and casual. "He's looking for a high-born noblewoman with good breeding and lots of money, and my dear Ella, I'm afraid you haven't got either."

I don't respond. Livia's specialty is being cruel for cruelty's sake. Her daughters are mostly just stupid, but Livia is *mean*.

"All right," she suddenly says. "You can go if you finish all your chores and make sure that Peyton and Slade are properly outfitted and ready first."

My mouth drops open.

"I can?" I say, astonished that Livia is being nice to me for once.

A smile crosses her face without reaching her eyes.

"Why not?" she says, and stands from her ugly-but-expensive chair and walks for the door. I'm just standing perfectly still, amazed that she said yes.

In the doorway, Livia turns back to me.

"Oh, Ella," she says. "You'll have to find something to wear."

Chapter Ten

Grayson

"Hi, welcome to Tremaine's—"

The hostess looks up at my face and stops short, the words dying on her lips.

"...Diner, how can I help you?" she finally finishes, her voice sounding a little dazed.

It's a reaction I get pretty often, being the prince and all. I smile at her.

"I've actually got a meeting with the manager," I say.

She just nods.

"Right. Of course, let me go see if Diane is here right now, I'll be right back can I get you coffee or water or anything? You can please feel free to sit at the bar and someone will be right along."

The words tumble nervously out of her mouth, and I give her my best royal smile.

"I'm quite all right, thank you," I say.

See? I know my manners sometimes.

"Be right back," she whispers, and then scurries off.

I wander to a display case full of pies and stand there for a long moment, peering in. They look okay as far as pies go: apple and banana creme and coconut and cherry, but my stomach is clenching inside me anyway.

The diner search hasn't turned up *shit*. I'm starting to think that I hallucinated this girl, because no diner's got an employment record of anyone who looks like her, not a single one in the entire city. It feels like I'm on some wild goose chase, only someone changed the rules and I have no idea what they are any more.

The ball is *tonight*, so this is my last chance to find her. After the ball, my father's decreed that I *narrow the pool*, starting with the women at the ball. And I can't imagine getting married to someone else, only to one day find the waitress.

"Hi. Excuse me?" it's the hostess again, and I turn. She's wringing her hands together in front of herself, looking so nervous she might jump out of her skin.

"Hi, sorry, so Diane isn't around right now but the owner is here? Livia Tremaine? Would you like to talk to her instead?"

I smile at the girl, because she seems nearly terrified of me. Any other time, I'd probably try to seduce her, but the thought just doesn't hold any appeal right now.

In fact, I haven't gotten laid since I first met the waitress. Nearly a week. It's my longest dry spell since I was a teenager, and it feels strange as hell.

"The owner would be just fine," I say.

The girl nods and leads me back, apologizing again and again as we walk through the kitchen and then a narrow, hot hallway, since it's the only way to Livia's office.

Just as I'm about to step through her office door,

something clicks. The Tremaine Diner *must* be the same Tremaine as Tremaine Holdings LLC, one of the biggest real estate developers in the city.

Gustav Tremaine, the guy who built the Tremaine empire from nothing, died about ten years ago. I was a kid, and I don't remember the details all that well, but it was something sudden and tragic. A car accident, I think. I do remember there was a scandal because he hadn't left a will, and after all the dust settled his second wife, who he'd only been married to for a few years, was in control of the company as well as all Gustav's assets.

Livia Tremaine is standing up when I walk in, behind a big ugly metal desk, and she curtsies with as much grace as her tiny space will allow her.

"Prince Grayson, Your Highness," she says. "Please accept my apologies for the state of the office, I didn't know I was expecting you today—"

I wave her off.

"I gave you no reason to expect me," I say, my tone formal and official.

"It's certainly an honor. Please, sit."

I follow her hand and sit in an office chair that's definitely seen better days.

"I'm looking for someone who I believe is an employee of yours," I say. "And while we've combed through your employee records, we've never managed to find this girl."

Livia's smiling at me, her teeth big and bright white, her hair bleach-blonde and perfectly waved on either side of her face, her eyelashes fake and her earrings huge. Everything about her screams *trophy wife*.

"What's her name?"

I fold my hands in my lap and lean back, exuding an aura of authority even in this dingy place.

"I'm not actually sure," I admit. "She wasn't wearing a name tag when she served me last week."

I could *swear* something in Livia's face changes, but I don't know what.

"Could you describe her?" Livia asks.

"Blonde hair, blue eyes. Heart-shaped face, about five-foot-four, I'd say. Very pretty, seemed a little shy. I'd like to make sure she's at the ball tomorrow night," I go on, trying to impress the importance of this mission onto Livia.

Her expression doesn't change. Her face doesn't move, not even the tiniest bit. Just a perfectly blank mask, which is strange.

"I don't think I employ anyone who matches that description," she says, and leans forward slightly. In doing so, she displays *just* the right amount of cleavage for the situation. "But, Your Highness, to be completely honest, I do have two employees who aren't on the books. Could it be one of them?"

I sit up a little straighter, my heart suddenly pounding. I'm close to finding her, I can *feel* it.

"Do they match the description?" I ask, trying not to sound too excited.

Livia pulls out her phone, giving me a coy look.

"I shouldn't be telling you this," she admits in a tone of voice that might work on another man, "but when employees call out sick, sometimes my daughters waitress under the table. This is them."

She holds out the phone, and I nearly grab it from her hand. On it is two pictures of two girls, but my heart sinks almost immediately. Her daughters are fine-looking, almost pretty, but neither of them is *the* waitress.

I just shake my head and hand the phone back, even though I've got the urge to fling it out the window. I swear I thought this was it, this was how I found her.

"Your daughters are lovely, but I'm afraid neither is the girl I'm looking for. Thanks for your time, Mrs. Tremaine," I say, and stand.

Her face still doesn't change as she curtsies again and I leave. On the way out, I want to punch the walls, the doors, everything that's seemingly standing in my way.

I don't know anything about this girl. I don't know why I want to find her so badly, but I do.

I want her. I need her.

And I'm going to find her, no matter what.

Chapter Eleven

Ella

"Hold *still*," I tell Slade as she ducks her head to check her phone for the fortieth time. I see her roll her eyes in the mirror, and I ignore it, pinning another curl into place.

This is the very last chore on the enormous list Livia gave me at the beginning of the week, and right now, I'm more nervous than a bunch of bees trapped in a box.

I haven't slept more than four hours a night since then. If I haven't been doing their bidding, I've been working on my dress for the ball, silently thanking the powers that be that I learned to sew as a kid.

It's not the fanciest dress, and it certainly wasn't the most expensive, but it's pretty and tasteful and meets the qualifications of a ball gown. Peyton was getting rid of a sapphire-blue dress that was "too last season," so I took it and made some changes.

It's one-shouldered and sparkly, with a skirt that flares out when I twirl, and I've got a really old pair of silver heels to wear with it.

At last, Slade and Peyton are ready. They fuss around for a while longer, demanding to know whether they look pretty or not, drinking champagne by the flute and touching up their lipstick.

I really, *really* want to go get ready myself. It won't take me that long, but I don't want to be too late to the ball.

But I also agreed not to leave before Slade and Peyton, who said that they don't want to walk in with me.

There are footsteps down the marble staircase, and the three of us turn to see Livia.

Wearing a blood-red ball gown, her hair up and makeup done.

"Mom, come *on*," Slade says, barely glancing at her mother.

I frown.

"You're going to the ball?" I ask.

Livia struts down the rest of the stairs, barely glancing my way. It's a chilly night, and she's got a fur stole around her shoulders.

"Of course I'm going," she says, her voice pure ice. "I'm eligible, aren't I?"

Her eyes meet mine, and an involuntary shiver moves through me.

"By the way, Ella," she says, turning toward the door. "Thank you for doing all those chores this week. Since you were so busy, I thought I'd help out by starting a load of laundry. There's a load of white sheets bleaching in the machine right now, along with those cleaning rags you had on that mannequin in your room."

Livia smiles with just her lips, and I'm shocked into silence. My dress was on the mannequin, the one I'm wearing tonight, and she just...

...My dress...

My mouth falls open, my vision blurring. I try to say something but I can't get any sound out of my mouth, but it doesn't matter because the three of them are sweeping out the door, and it closes behind them with an ominous *thud*.

On autopilot, I walk to my room. Tears are rolling down my cheeks, but I barely even feel them as I rush towards the servants' wing, even though I already know what I'm going to find.

My hands are shaking as I open the washing machine.

There, on top, is my dress. Or what *was* my dress.

She bleached it into an ugly, mottled gray-blue, but that's not all. My dress is a horrible color, but even worse, it's cut into pieces. Little strips, about an inch wide.

I just stare. After this last week, of getting almost no sleep and working my fingers to the bone all for this one tiny spark of hope, all I can do is stare.

How could I think she was actually going to be nice to me? I wonder numbly. *How could I be so gullible?*

Slowly, I shut the lid of the washing machine. I walk back into my room.

And then I lay on my bed and cry.

• • •

Fifteen minutes later, my phone buzzes.

Flynn: How's the ball?

I take a deep breath and wonder if I should just lie, because I don't feel like going into it with Flynn. But he'll get the truth out of me eventually anyway, so there's no point.

Me: I'm not there.
Flynn: What?
Me: She didn't let me go.

Almost instantly, my phone rings. It's Flynn, and before I've even said anything he's yelling.

"What do you *mean* she didn't let you? You did everything she asked! You made that dress! You refinished the floors and cleaned out the garage!"

I take a deep breath, try not to cry, and tell him the story. When I finish, there's a long, long pause on the other end of the line, so long I think he's gone.

"Flynn?" I ask.

"I'm here," he says, his voice sounding far away. "And you know what? Ella, I got this."

"You've got *what*?"

"This fucked-up situation. Fuck Livia and fuck her bitch-ass daughters, you held up your end of the bargain."

"It doesn't *matter*," I sigh.

"Like hell it doesn't. Ella, go take a shower and grab your best foundation garments, because I'm gonna be there in twenty minutes."

Flynn hangs up without waiting for a response, and I'm left lying on my bed, staring at my phone.

Slowly, I sit up. I dry my eyes.

And, wondering what the hell Flynn thinks he's doing, I head into the shower.

Chapter Twelve

Grayson

I hate these damned things.

I've never liked balls. Not for a second, not even because they usually afford me a chance at a veritable *buffet* of women. They're too straight-laced for me, too formal. There are tons of social rules and guidelines that I have to follow, and I've learned the hard way what happens when I *don't* follow them.

My father happens is what.

A dance ends. I bow to the girl I was dancing with, and she curtsies. There's a hopeful look in her eyes but I'm already glancing away as the music fades, scanning the crowd at the edges of the dance floor for the waitress.

She's not there. I've been looking for her all night, but I haven't seen her, and since this ball is being thrown in my honor, it's been hard for me to escape the dance floor.

"Thank you," I tell my dance partner, but before she can even open her mouth to respond, I'm gone, walking briskly from the dance floor and toward a hallway. I don't care if it's just to the bathroom, I need to get out of here for five minutes and catch my breath.

"Your Highness," an older man says, stepping into my path. He's got steel-gray hair and he's holding both his hands out, palms up, like he's showing off a jewelry case full of expensive watches.

"Lord Graviston," I answer, slowing without stopping.

"I don't believe I've had the pleasure of introducing you to my daughter and my niece," he begins, but I smile and hold up one hand.

"I'm so sorry, you've caught me in a moment of need," I say. It would be more polite to simply stay and chat to the daughters — both kind of pretty, but plain — but I don't think I can handle one more courteous statement right now.

He smiles beseechingly.

"Apologies, Your Highness," he says. "Perhaps I can introduce you later."

I nod, then keep walking away, toward the VIP restrooms. Of course we have them. It's a palace, and my family and I aren't about to wait in a line to pee.

I walk through a hall, open a door, and nod at a guard who opens the door into the VIP bathroom lounge for me.

And I stop dead in my tracks.

My sister and Declan are sitting on a couch together, and she's *laughing*. Clearly, it's at something he's said, because she's got one hand over her mouth, her cheeks bright pink and her eyes dancing.

Hell no. Hell fucking goddamn *no*, Declan can't be in here alone making my little sister laugh. I know what

Declan got up to last weekend — the phrase "could suck a golf ball through a garden hose" was used in a text — and there is no *way* he's getting anywhere near Aurora.

"Grayson!" my sister exclaims, still laughing. "You never told me that Declan has an amazing impression of Lord Whiffleboff."

The guard, who's still holding the door, clears his throat politely. I step forward and he lets the door swing closed, leaving the three of us alone.

"I didn't know Declan had an amazing impression of Lord Whiffleboff," I say, keeping my voice as neutral and even as I possibly can.

"It's really good," she says, still laughing, but neither of us are really paying attention to her. I'm glaring daggers at Declan, and he's glaring right back.

If you touch her I'll murder you, I think, hoping he gets the message.

I don't care what kingdom you're heir to, if you so much as touch my little sister I'll hunt you down and murder you.

"Come on, show Grayson," Aurora says, lightly resting her fingertips on Declan's shoulder.

I nearly explode. Yeah, I'm a fucking hypocrite, given that I behave just as badly as he does, but I don't care.

If I find his filthy paws on my sister, I'll kill him. I will.

"I don't know if I can do it on command," Declan says, finally breaking our glare-off and looking over at Aurora. "If it's going to be any good it needs to be spontaneous."

"Please?" Aurora asks, tilting her head just a little.

Declan shakes his head.

"Fine," she says, rolling her eyes teasingly. "Well, if you get the urge to *spontaneously* make fun of any of my father's other cranky old advisors, you'll come find me, won't you?"

"Of course," Declan responds.

Aurora smiles at him, then stands.

"Mother is probably searching for me right now," she says. "You know how she is, 'Never too early to start considering a match,' like, jeez Mom, can I be old enough to legally drink first? Bye!"

With that, my little sister practically bounces from the room, a ray of sunshine just like her name.

I snap my head back toward Declan, who holds up both palms.

"I didn't touch her," he says. "She was in here when I came in, we chatted for a little while, that's it. You know your whole family is practically my family too, Aurora's like my little sister."

I almost say *sure, your little sister who just got back from boarding school all grown up*, but I don't. Declan may not respect very many rules, but I'm pretty sure he'll respect this one.

"Anyone but my sister," I say, leveling one finger at him. "Seriously, Declan. One hand on her and I'll light you on fire."

"As far as I'm concerned, Aurora's still got cooties," he says.

"Good."

"See you out on the dance floor?" he asks, and I nod. Declan leaves, and now I've got the whole lounge to myself.

I'm not stupid. I've got eyes, and I've noticed that not only is my little sister gorgeous, she attracts her fair share of male attention.

But fucking Declan. He's my best friend, but that means I know exactly what he's been up to. He doesn't date or fall in love. The most he does is fuck women twice before he gets tired of them.

And I want better for my little sister. Way fucking better.

I sigh, push my hand through my hair, and go into the men's to take a piss.

Maybe the waitress will be there when I get back.

Chapter Thirteen

Ella

"All right, here we are," Flynn says, and the car stops.

I pull the cooling mask he brought me off my eyes and look through the windshield, but it doesn't clear much up. All I see is a big, windowless building that says *Hot Lips* on the side in screamingly pink neon.

"Where's *here*?" I ask, totally baffled. "Is being a stripper really my only option if I can't go to the ball?"

"*The Hot Lips Lounge* is a classy establishment, thank you very much," he says. "And congratulations, girl, after weeks of asking you're finally about to meet Thomas."

And *now* it all makes sense. Flynn's new boyfriend Thomas moonlights as Charlize LaCroix, one of the most in-demand drag performers in the kingdom. Or, at least, that's what Flynn says. I'm not really up on the drag scene, to be honest.

"Wait," I say. "Am I borrowing a dress from

Thomas? I thought you said he was six feet tall and a former linebacker."

Flynn grins at me, opening his car door.

"He is, and every inch of that body is glorious," he says. "But if I know one person who can work his magic and get you looking *right* for this ball, it's him. You coming, or what?"

I follow Flynn into the Hot Lips Lounge without another word. The bouncer at the door nods at Flynn, and then we're inside.

On stage, there's a woman — well, a drag queen — strutting back and forth and lip synching to a song I've never heard before, but the crowd is going absolutely insane for her.

And honestly, it's impressive. I think I'd die of stage fright if I had to do anything like that, and this queen not only has stage presence, but she's an amazing dancer. In five-inch heels.

Flynn leans over to me.

"That's my boo," he says proudly, and my mouth drops open.

"She can do anything she wants to me!" I say.

· · ·

Fifteen minutes later, I'm sitting on an overturned milk crate backstage, and Charlize LaCroix is leaning one elbow on a vanity, looking at me.

"She cut your dress up *and* bleached it?" she says, her red lips an O of astonishment. "That's not just overkill, she sounds like a straight-up psychopath. What on earth are you still doing there, girl?"

I open my mouth to go into the whole 'legal custodian' thing, but Flynn cuts me off.

"I'll explain it later, but I'm with you there," he says,

standing behind me, arms crossed. "I've told her a thousand times, she can come sleep on my couch until she figures something out instead of babysitting two grown-ass morons and living with the Wicked Witch herself. But right now, we've got to get her to this ball. She's already an hour late."

Charlize looks at me thoughtfully, tapping one long fake red nail against the countertop.

"I'll have to see if I can borrow a few things," she says. "You're not exactly my size or my skin tone, sweetheart."

"If you can't, it's no big—"

Charlize just laughs.

"Who said *can't*?" she says, standing. "You're gonna leave here looking like the finest piece of princess-to-be ass that Prince Grayson has seen in his damn life. Let me change outta this mess and I'll get started on you."

Charlize takes her wig off and plops it onto a mannequin head, then grabs a pile of clothes and walks behind a screen.

"By the way, when the wig is on I'm Charlize, but when it's off I'm Thomas," he says. "Plan your statements accordingly."

Flynn chuckles as Thomas's sparkly red dress flops over the top of the screen, followed shortly by hose, a bra, garters, a corset, and undergarments I don't even recognize.

After a moment, Thomas walks out in basketball shorts and a Tremaine's Diner t-shirt, pulling his fake eyelashes off. It's a little strange to see a huge, in-shape guy still wearing lipstick, blush, and more eyeshadow than I've owned in my entire life, but I go with it.

"All right," he says, eyeing me up and down. "Stand up, give us a twirl, and tell me your measurements."

• • •

There's a pinprick in my back, and I gasp.

"Sorry, sweetie," Thomas murmurs. "Almost done. Flynn, can you hold this any tighter?"

My new dress tightens around me, and I hold my breath. It's a surprisingly understated dress for one I got from a drag show, but it's blue, shimmery, and when it moves it catches the light in a way that makes my breath catch.

They haven't let me look in the mirror yet, though, so I've got no clue whether I look normal or like I've been dressed by a drag queen.

"All right," Thomas finally says, releasing my dress and stepping back. "Time to turn around."

I do.

Then I gasp, both my hands flying to my mouth, because I look *amazing* in this dress. I don't know whose it is or where Thomas found it, but it fits me perfectly — or at least it does now, with a line of safety pins going up my back.

It's shimmery blue, the front low cut enough to show just a hint of cleavage without going overboard. It hugs my waist, dips low in the back, and somehow makes my butt look incredible.

I just stand there, open-mouthed, staring at myself.

"Well, how fabulous am I?" Thomas asks, grinning, arms crossed over his chest.

"So fabulous," I breathe. "How did you *do* this?"

"I told you he was magic," Flynn says.

"Baby, you said that?" Thomas asks.

"You know I did."

They kiss quickly while I stare at myself, still blown away. As someone who hardly ever wears make up and only owns two skirts, I can't believe I'm actually looking at myself in the mirror.

"The prince ain't gonna know what hit him," Thomas says. "But there's one more thing."

Panic stabs through my heart. My makeup's done, my hair is up, and I look way better than I ever have in my life.

Thomas disappears again, and I trade a glance with Flynn.

"What's the one more thing?" I ask.

He looks me up and down.

"Shoes, girl," he says. "You can't go in there barefoot."

Thomas comes back into the dressing room, then steps up to me and holds out a pair of shoes.

Shoes is an understatement. These are something more than shoes, because every millimeter except the sole is totally covered in sparkling white crystal. Every time they move they shine like a disco ball, and my mouth drops open yet again.

"These are all I could find that might fit you," he says. "Women's size seven isn't too common among drag queens."

He's got a point. I take the shoes, put them on the ground, and step into them, praying.

They fit. *Perfectly.* They're not even too high, and they stay on my feet even after I take a few steps, carefully holding my skirt up.

"I think we did great," Flynn says to Thomas.

"I think maybe we should get to go to the ball just to see how great we did," Thomas says. "Give me ninety minutes and Charlize LaCroix can be in attendance. Though she'd probably steal the prince away for her very own, so scratch that."

He winks at me. I'm just grinning like an idiot,

because even though this ball is probably stupid and the prince won't look at me twice, I'm really excited to get my way despite Livia.

"Thanks, guys," I say. "I don't know how I can return the favor."

"Return it by leaving that witch behind and sleeping on my couch," Flynn says.

Chapter Fourteen

Grayson

Every time I turn around at this damned ball, there's another eligible bachelorette standing there, looking at me with big does eyes, like she's just waiting for me to lose my mind and fall in love with her.

They're not all ugly. They're not even all bad-looking. Some are pretty hot, exactly the kind of girl I'd have gone after a few weeks ago.

But they're never the waitress. Not even once.

And it's a little past ten, meaning no new guests are arriving at this ball.

She's not here. She's not coming. This ball has been the talk of the entire kingdom for a week now, so the only way she didn't come is if she didn't want to.

But still, I can't stop thinking about her. The way she looked at me, the way her lips moved when she spoke. Her ass under her uniform as she walked away, or even better, when she bent over a table to clear dishes.

I keep dancing with other girls at this ball because I have to, but I'm just thinking about the waitress. Her pretty lips around my cock, the taste of her in my mouth.

All the ways I could *take* her and make her moan. What I wouldn't give to feel her tight, hot wetness around my cock while she screamed my name.

I head over to the bar, but it doesn't help. The second I have a drink in my hand, someone new wants my attention.

"Your Highness," says a woman's voice, and I turn.

It's the Duchess of Montagne, who's broad, tall, and shall we say a very *commanding* presence.

"Duchess," I say, nodding my head slightly as she curtsies.

"Have you had the pleasure of meeting my daughters yet tonight?" she goes on, still imperious-sounding as ever.

"I've not," I say, taking a sip of my scotch. I'm vaguely familiar with her daughters — all six of them — but I've never been able to keep them straight or even come anywhere close to remembering their names. It doesn't help that they all start with R.

"This is Rachelle," she starts. "Twenty-seven, *quite* marriageable. She'll be inheriting most of her father's fortune and her monthly courses are exceedingly regular, which bodes well for her fecundity—"

Rachelle instantly turns bright red and looks at the floor, not that her mother notices.

"—She's still a virgin, our family doctor checks her hymen annually—"

Rachelle closes her eyes, and I can't help but feel completely awful for her, and I'm about to interrupt her mother just to spare the poor girl, when a flash of blue catches my eye, and I stop.

For the first time in over an hour, someone's entering the ballroom. It's someone new, someone who's never been here before, judging by the way she looks around as she opens the huge, heavy door and peeks in.

Right away, the doormen scurry over. One holds the door open, and the other bows to her, taking her hand and welcoming her to the ball.

I can't see her face, but somehow, I *know* it's her. I just do. It's like she lights up the entire room just by entering it.

The Duchess is still talking, but I have no idea what she's saying. I walk past her in a trance, handing her my drink, making my way toward the waitress who's still looking around, half overwhelmed and half bewildered.

Watching her, I can barely breathe. She's in a shimmering blue dress that shows off every curve of her incredible body flawlessly, from her full, perky breasts, to the notch of her waist to the curve of her ass that's just *made* for grabbing.

Already, I want to tear it off of her. I want to pin her against the wall, throw her legs over my shoulders, rip off her panties and taste her right here, right now, and I don't give a single damn that everyone is watching.

As I move toward her, she catches my eye and stops. Just freezes, right here in the middle of the ball. I can feel all eyes on me, everyone at this thing wondering who the hell this girl that *I'm* approaching could possibly be, but I don't care.

The waitress came. I found her again, and there's absolutely nothing that's going to stand in the way of me making her mine.

She turns toward me as I approach, and I smile at her, holding out my hand. She swallows, just barely licking her bottom lip as she does, and I swear I go rock-hard in a second.

The waitress puts her hand in mine, still staring at me, wide-eyed. I think she's holding her breath, until at the very last second, she remembers to curtsy.

I kiss her hand, soft and delicate. Just like her.

"May I have this dance?" I ask.

Chapter Fifteen

Ella

I have a theory about all this.

I think I'm on drugs.

It's the only thing that makes any sense. A week ago, right before Prince Grayson and his friends walked into my diner and ordered breakfast, someone must have drugged me. Maybe Flynn, maybe Livia, maybe the other waitress working that day, I don't know.

But they drugged me, and then I met the prince. And then the prince propositioned me in the diner, and I ran away, and now I'm hallucinating everything about tonight: Livia ruining my dress, Flynn saving me, Charlize/Thomas outfitting me, the whole nine yards.

And now I'm hallucinating Prince Grayson smiling at me and kissing my hand. I'm hallucinating him asking me to dance while *every other woman in the entire kingdom* stares at the two of us.

I'm hallucinating the band striking up a waltz, one

of his hands on my waist and the other in mine as he leads me across the dance floor. Thank *God* my father paid for dancing lessons for me before he died.

"I didn't think you were going to come," he says as we start whirling around the dance floor.

That takes me by surprise.

"You thought about whether I was going to come?" I ask, the words out of my mouth before I can think of something better to say.

Step, step, whirl.

"I did," he says. "I've been trying to find you ever since you turned me down at the diner."

My stomach clenches, and I feel the heat rush to my face. I look away, over his shoulder, at the champagne fountain on the far side of the ballroom.

Prince Grayson just laughs.

"I threw a fucking *ball* to find you, and I don't even know your name," he goes on, whirling me again. "I've thought about almost nothing for a week except ten thousand ways to make you orgasm, and I don't even know your name."

I clear my throat, my face even hotter. Something *else* is hot too, something liquid and writhing deep inside me. No one has ever talked to me like this before, and... I think I like it.

"It's Ella," I say.

"Ella. Beautiful," he says. "Too beautiful to be working as a breakfast waitress."

"Someone's got to do it, haven't they?" I ask, finally finding my voice. "I won't be a breakfast waitress forever."

"Tell me, Ella," he says. "What do you do when you're not a breakfast waitress?"

I think for a moment. Besides Flynn and now Thomas, no one really knows about my weird situation.

Working so much and then coming home just to work more kind of puts a damper on my social life, to say the least, and I'm always wary of what people will think.

"I'm a housekeeper," I say lightly. "I work for a noble family with two daughters."

For some reason, Prince Grayson just grins at that, and suddenly, I'm embarrassed.

"My father died when I was young and I had to make my way in the world early," I say, getting defensive. "I did finish high school, and I just haven't had a chance to go to college or anything yet, but I'd like to."

"I wasn't laughing at you," he murmurs. "I was laughing at the fact that I threw an entire ball to find a girl who's a part time waitress, part time housekeeper while every duchess in the kingdom is practically launching her daughters at me."

"That sounds dangerous," I say without thinking.

"What does?"

The music is slowing now, the song coming to a close. Prince Grayson pulls me a little closer, his hand tightening on my waist.

"Having women launched at you," I say.

"Don't worry, I can handle myself just fine," he murmurs, pulling me closer again.

Now our bodies are pressed together, much closer than a waltz dictates, and suddenly I can feel his heat through his formal outfit.

Not only that, I can feel something *else,* something thick and hard and massive pressing against my belly, and it takes me a moment to realize what it is.

At the exact moment that I realize what's happening, Prince Grayson leans down, his lips close to my ear. I can feel virtually everyone else in this ballroom staring at us.

But as he whispers, shivers run up and down my back. A river of fire flows through me, and I remember *why* I came.

I came because for a week I've been getting myself off, fingers inside my tight channel wishing it was *him*.

I came because, to my amazement, I regret not letting Prince Grayson bend me over the bathroom sink at work and take my virginity right then and there.

And I came because my life is dull and boring, punctuated by moments of stupidity and cruelty from my family, and this is for me. I want to do something sexy and exciting, something that *I* want to do for once.

I want the prince, and no one and nothing can stop me.

"Ella," he says, his lips brushing my ear as my eyes slide closed. "May I have another dance?"

Chapter Sixteen

Grayson

We dance again and again. Other people try to cut in, but I simply refuse them.

Ella came, and I'm going to dance with her. It's as simple as that.

When I don't think I can dance another step, I take her hand and lead her from the dance floor. Though the crowd is thinning, various people — a Countess, an Earl, a Baron — try to get my attention, but I brush them off as politely as I can.

This will be all over the tabloids tomorrow, but I don't really give a shit. *Prince Grayson Dances Several Times with Same Woman* won't upset even my father as a headline.

We're nearly out of the ballroom when yet another pompous nobleman steps into my way.

"Your Highness," he begins. "Allow me to introduce my daughter, Lady Ardana of..."

Suddenly, Ella's hand tightens in mine. I look over at her, the nobleman still chattering away about his daughter, and Ella is rigid, her whole body tense, and she's staring at the other end of the ballroom.

There's a woman staring right back, and she sends a sharp tingle of recognition through me, though I'm having trouble placing her. She's flanked by two younger women who are both fiddling with their hair and staring down at their phones, but the older woman in the middle is just *watching* Ella.

And Ella is motionless, staring right back. Alarm bells are going off in my head, because even though I don't know why they're staring at each other, I don't like the way this woman's looking at Ella.

My Ella.

I straighten my spine. I'm no longer even pretending to listen to this nobleman prattle on and on, I'm just full-force glaring back at this woman, tightening my hand on Ella's.

"It's an honor, Your Highness," another woman's voice says, and I finally turn.

A girl — probably the nobleman's daughter, though I've clearly not been paying attention — curtsies very, *very* low, giving me a view straight down her cleavage.

I don't even glance, I just nod at her.

"Likewise," I say, and turn away with Ella.

"Who is that?" I growl when we're out of earshot.

Ella just shakes her head, her cheeks turning faintly pink. Rage simmers inside me, though I don't quite understand why.

"Don't worry about it," she says, her voice soft and gentle.

"I'm going to go have a word with her," I say, and start for the woman.

"Please don't!" Ella says, grabbing my hand in both

of hers.

I stop. People around us are watching us like hawks, but I ignore them.

"I'm having such a nice time," she says, her blue eyes searching mine. "Can't we just leave the ball like we were going to and go..."

Ella turns *bright* pink, all the way from her collarbones to her forehead, and I swallow hard. His Royal Hardness is suddenly at full mast, so rigid and insistent that I can practically feel the seams on these pants ripping open.

Instantly, I've forgotten about the blonde woman, and I smirk at Ella, pulling her closer in to me. My hard cock brushes up against her, and the sensation sends a tremble through my whole body.

"Go where?" I whisper, teasing her.

She swallows, looking down.

"I just thought... somewhere else?" she whispers. "Somewhere that we could be alone?"

She doesn't have to ask twice. I practically barrel for the doors, knocking nobles out of my way left and right. I'm already thinking about the things I'm going to do to this perfect, luscious girl, the way I'm going to make her sigh and scream my name, and I don't give a damn who hears.

I push open the massive door, pull Ella through, and shut it behind us. The doormen stare, and though I have the urge to kiss her right then and there, I fight it because I don't want our first kiss to be with two of my father's servants gawking at me.

There's a small, private hallway off the foyer, and I lead Ella in there, away from their eyes.

She gasps as I spin her around, take her by the waist, and push her against the wall.

"Is this why you came to the ball?" I murmur,

pressing my body against hers.

She's panting for breath, her perfect pink lips parted. Her tongue slides along the inside of her top lip, an unconscious gesture that makes my dick nearly explode.

"Is what why?"

"Because you wanted to take me up on my offer from last week," I say, stroking her hip through the sparkling fabric with one hand. "Though now that you're here, I plan on making this *anything* but quick."

"I hadn't forgotten," she whispers. "But, Your Highness—"

"Grayson."

"I wasn't expecting this, I just came because it seemed like it would be fun, I really didn't think you'd remember."

I just chuckle.

"Well, I did remember," I say, letting my lips graze her ear. "I remember the way you bit your lip when you took our order. I remember how hard I got watching your ass when you bent over the table. I remember wanting to hear you moan as you rode my cock, right there in the booth."

I bite her ear gently, and she gasps.

"And I remember you turning me down so I had to fantasize about sinking my cock into your sweet little pussy for a week straight."

Ella moves her hips against me unconsciously, and that's all it takes.

I bend down and press my lips to hers, claiming her sweet, pink mouth. She kisses me back, her hands on my shoulders, her lips needy and hungry in a way that lights a nuclear fire inside me.

I swipe my tongue along her lower lip, and she moans softly as she opens her mouth and I plunder her with my tongue, tasting her, *taking* her. I kiss Ella nearly hard enough to bruise her but she kisses me back just as fiercely, her body moving against mine with an intensity that makes me think I might lose my mind.

I run one hand up her side, feeling her warm body under her dress, the curve of her breast swelling with each breath. It's almost more than I can take.

I need her here, *now*, and I don't care who knows what we're doing. I skim my thumb over one nipple, through the fabric, and even through her bra I feel it stiffen under my hand.

"Ella," I whisper into her ear. "I'm going to make you come so hard you forget your own name, and I'm going to do it right here in this hallway."

Ella freezes suddenly, holding her breath.

"Wait," she whispers. "Grayson."

"What?" I ask, kissing her neck, her collarbone.

All I can think about is getting on my knees in front of this perfect, beautiful girl. Licking her sweet pussy and tasting her until she comes completely undone.

Ella clears her throat. She clears it again, until I stop and look up at her.

"I'm a virgin," she says.

Chapter Seventeen

Ella

I shouldn't have said anything, because now Grayson is just staring at me. Like I'm some sort of swamp monster or alien or something.

He probably would have figured it out when I didn't know what I was doing, but I could have faked it for a while. I've seen movies, I've used a vibrator, I'm not a total idiot.

I'm just... inexperienced.

"Say it again," he commands.

I close my eyes and lean my head against the wall, biting my lip.

"I'm a virgin," I whisper.

"Again."

"I'm a virgin?"

His lips are back on me, moving from my collarbone down my chest, along the fairly low neckline of my dress.

"Good," he says. "Because I want to be the first man to taste you."

Grayson reaches under my dress, through the open back, and unhooks my strapless bra with one hand, pulling it out and tossing it into a corner.

"I want to be the first man to hear you moan as I pleasure you," he says, taking a nipple in his teeth through my dress.

I gasp, my hands on his head, in his hair.

"I want to be the first man to undress you, taste your sweet honey, and fuck you with my tongue while you come," he murmurs.

My toes curl in my shoes. No one's ever talked to me this way, and I never imagined that anyone would, but my panties are soaked completely through right now. I can feel myself absolutely throbbing with desire, and the lower he moves, the more I *want* him.

"And I want to be the first man to feel you come while I fuck your sweet little pussy," he finishes.

I'm speechless. I have no idea how to respond to that — what do I say, *sounds good?* — But Grayson is already on his knees in front of me, his hands squeezing and kneading my breasts, rolling my nipples between his fingers.

I moan, despite myself, and he chuckles, his mouth grazing my lower belly, my hip, and then at last, his lips brushing over my mound, all through my dress.

I wobble in my sparkly shoes, and he pushes his hands up my dress, along my legs, until he reaches my panties. Then he tugs them down until they're around my ankles, and I wobble again trying to get them off.

The moment they're in the corner, next to my discarded bra, Grayson's fingers are stroking up my inner thigh, brushing the crease where it meets my hip. His fingers are rough and gentle, all at once, and he slides them between my folds while I'm still standing, instantly finding my pleasure button.

I just grab his hair a little harder and hold on, head thrown back, biting my lip, and I swear he *growls*.

"You like that, kitten?" he murmurs, his fingers moving faster in my slick wetness.

"Yes," I gasp out, even though I can't *believe* I'm doing this.

Grayson shoves my skirt up higher, and now he's holding it up over my hips. I'm totally exposed, in this small hallway inside the Royal Palace, the only thing covering the crown prince's face.

"You like being touched in public," he says, his voice low, dangerous, and inches from my pussy. "You're so fucking wet for me, kitten, and I want to lick every drop of honey from your sweet little cunt."

I just moan. Ten minutes ago I'd have been shocked that someone said that to me, but right now I just want more. More of his fingers, more of his tongue, more of... *him*.

"Please, Grayson," I whimper.

He chuckles, and suddenly I feel his tongue on me, sliding into my cleft, and I force myself to loosen my grip on his hair as I turn my head to one side.

Don't make too much noise, I remind myself. *Everyone will be able to hear you...*

Suddenly, Grayson grabs one leg and hoists it over his shoulder, spreading my thighs apart right in front of his face. I gasp, wobbling on the other leg, but his strong, firm hands keep me upright even as he groans in pleasure.

Instantly, his tongue is on my clit, flicking it in a slow, lazy circle as his fingers stroke my dripping entrance, gently moving back and forth across my swollen, drooling lips.

I forget where I am, or that I'm standing on a single high heel. I forget absolutely everything except the prince's mouth on me and how fucking *incredible* it feels.

"Grayson," I whisper. "Oh my God, that feels so good."

He licks me harder, faster, his tongue working total magic on me as his finger slide between my wet lips, teasing me even more. I bite my lip almost hard enough to draw blood, because I want to scream.

I want to beg him to fuck me right here, right now. I want him to stretch me with his fingers and then I want him to bend me over and take me hard and deep standing against this wall. I don't care that everyone in the ballroom can probably hear us, and I don't care that the doormen right outside almost certainly know what's going on in here.

One finger enters me, slowly, gently, and Grayson strokes the sensitive front wall of my pussy with it, in time with his tongue.

It feels so good I nearly scream, one fist to my mouth so I don't make too much noise.

"Please," I beg. "Please, Grayson, *please*."

I don't even know what exactly I'm asking him to do, I just know that I'm wound up and nearly desperate.

All at once, his finger inside me bends in a way that makes me arch my back and roll my eyes at the exact same time that he closes his lips around my clit and sucks on it.

I feel like fireworks go off inside me, slowly at first but building and building until they crescendo and I have to bite my fist to keep from screaming Grayson's name while he licks me and fucks me, still standing there in the hallway.

When it's over, tremors are still moving through my body. I've still got my head back against the wall, my eyes closed, and I'm panting for breath with my lips slightly parted.

Grayson stands, letting the skirt of my dress fall to the floor. When I open my eyes, he's grinning, and he takes my hand and kisses it.

Holy shit, the prince just ate me out in public, I think, and the reminder stuns me so much that I'm speechless.

I feel like I should run, maybe without even telling him goodbye. I can't believe I did that — me, nice girl, waitress and housekeeper Ella.

And I can't believe I want to do it *again*.

"You're fucking beautiful," Grayson says. "I could lick your pussy for ten hours straight, kitten."

Despite everything, I feel myself blush.

"I liked that," I whisper, and he just grins.

"Good," he says. "Because we're just getting started."

And with that, he takes my hand and pulls me along the hallway, leaving my bra and panties behind.

Chapter Eighteen

Grayson

I don't even wait for the door to my chambers to close before I'm claiming her mouth again with my own, thrusting my tongue deeply inside her. I can still smell her honey on myself, and the smell only turns me on even more.

"Ella," I growl.

She runs her hands lightly down my chest, her lips swollen from our kisses, almost like she's not quite sure what to do next.

Ella has an innocence about her that I find utterly intoxicating. Like every time she hesitates I want her more, want to show her what to do, bend her to my will.

I grab her ass. I pull her against me roughly, my thick, throbbing erection against her lower belly as she bites her lip and moans quietly.

"You're so fucking beautiful," I say, my voice low

and rough. "And you're going to be mine, kitten."

"Make me yours," she whispers, blinking up at me through her long eyelashes as her hands come to rest on my belt. "Please."

In response, I run my hands up her body, grabbing her breasts through the shimmering blue fabric, sliding my hands over her nipples as they stiffen. Ella's eyes drift closed with pleasure and I squeeze a little harder, pinching her nipples a little more roughly.

She *moans* and slides her hand lightly down the front of my trousers, along the length of my cock, and I swear lightning passes through my entire body that I can't control. I kiss her again, tugging on the neckline of her dress, moving it down her flushed, creamy skin until one rosy nipple pops out.

I run my thumb across it roughly, and Ella moans into my mouth, the sound driving me even wilder as she melts into me. I move my lips from her mouth along her jaw, to the soft, delectable skin of her neck, still rolling her nipple between my fingers as I walk her backward, across the room.

In a few moments, we're at a huge leather couch. On the wall opposite one end is an enormous, gilt-edged dressing mirror. Ella stumbles for a moment as her feet hit the couch, but in a moment, I've lifted her, shoved her against the back and I'm kneeling underneath her.

I pull on her dress again and her other nipple pops out, dusky pink and fucking perfect, just begging to be sucked and licked so I take it into my mouth, teasing it with my tongue, still playing with her other nipple.

Ella's straddling me, her legs wrapped around my back, and as I suck and lick her she sighs, squeezing me tighter and rolling her hips against my thick shaft. I groan and bite her nipple a little harder, glancing in the mirror as I do.

God, she's fucking beautiful. She's even more beautiful like this, half-undone, letting me pleasure her like the dirty girl she is as she gasps and moans.

I lick her nipple one last time and she gasps, bucking her hips against me wildly, like she's lost all self-control. I'm completely utterly, *impossibly* hard and every time she grinds her heat against me I think I might just come right then and there, it feels so good.

"You like feeling your wet little pussy against my cock?" I ask before taking her nipple in my teeth again.

Ella pauses, panting for breath.

"Yes," she finally whispers.

"You're so wet you're about to soak straight through the fabric," I go on, releasing her nipple from my teeth. "Tell me, should I make you come again?"

She just nods, breathless, and I pull her dress down again by the neck. Something tears, but suddenly Ella is undressed to the waist, her perfect, small-but-full breasts heaving in front of me. I can't fucking help myself. I suck one nipple into my mouth, then the other, leaving them even pinker and puffier.

Ella gasps and moans, winding her fingers through my hair.

"Grayson," she whimpers. "That feels so good."

I flick my tongue across one and look up at her, still grinding her against my cock because she's so fucking delicious that I can't help myself.

"Tell me what you want me to do to you," I growl. "I want to hear it from your pretty little mouth."

Her eyes pop open, and she swallows before putting one hand on my chest.

"I want you to..."

She trails off, like she's suddenly shy even though she's half naked on my lap. I slide one hand up her thigh until I can stroke her wetness with one thumb, and she bites her lip in pleasure.

"You want me to stroke your tight little pussy until you come?" I ask.

She nods, her chest still rising and falling tantalizingly.

"You want me to put my fingers inside you?" I go on.

She nods, wordless. I lean in until my lips are almost on her ear.

"You want me to fuck you deep with my thick, hard cock?"

Ella shivers so hard I can feel it, her nipples stiffening against my chest as she swallows hard.

"Yes," she finally whispers.

"Say it."

"I want you to..."

I bite her ear, and she gasps.

"Fuck me," she whispers quickly.

I bite harder.

I barely know this girl, but I *need* her. I want to be her first, and suddenly, I know she's going to be my last.

I slide my fingers between her lips, stroking her slick entrance, and she moans again.

"I can't wait to be your first, kitten," I whisper.

Chapter Nineteen

Ella

I lean backward against the couch, letting Grayson stroke me. My dress is half off, I'm pretty sure it's ruined, and I can't *believe* I'm half-dressed on a couch with the crown prince who I barely know, but everything feels so good that I don't care.

"Please," I whisper, though I don't even know what I'm asking.

I'm so wound up that I want him right now, I want to slide down the zipper of his pants, pull out his cock, and slide him deep inside my virgin pussy until he makes me come again.

And I think I want it more than I've ever wanted *anything*.

"Please what?" he growls, teasing, one thumb circling my clit.

I shift my hips again, bucking them against the cock I so desperately want.

"Please fuck me," I say, my voice a barely-audible whisper.

In a flash, Grayson is standing and pulling me off the couch. He kisses me roughly, pushing my dress the rest of the way off. There's another tearing sound, but as soon as I'm completely naked in front of him I'm somehow back on the couch, only this time I'm on all fours.

There's a massive mirror across from me, and I'm looking at myself over the arm of the couch. Grayson is standing beside me, still totally clothed, and he leans down to kiss me as he runs one hand along my spine, from my neck to my lower back.

But he doesn't stop. I gasp as his finger moves down the cleft between my ass cheeks, right over the sensitive ring there, but then his hand is on my pussy again, his fingers teasing at my opening.

I feel so exposed, so vulnerable, but as he pushes one finger inside and strokes my inner wall, I don't care anymore.

"You've got a tight little pussy," he growls, pushing his finger further in.

I tighten my hands on the leather of the couch. Even though it's just one finger, it still feels *so* good, especially as he moves it inside me against all my most sensitive parts.

"More," I gasp.

"Greedy," he chides me, his other hand stroking slowly up my back, but he pulls his hand back and then adds a second finger, fucking me slowly, and I gasp.

Now it feels really good, like I'm filled up, and I rock backward on my hands and knees, taking him all the way up to his knuckles, moaning for more.

"That's right, I want to see you fuck me like the dirty girl you are," Grayson says, crooking both his fingers at once inside me.

I just moan, pushing my hips back again. I need *more* of him, and I need him deeper, now, as he runs his other hand through my hair and then grabs a handful, pulling my head back just slightly.

"Do you want more?" he asks softly, though his voice is filled with control and lust.

He's standing next to me, the entire outline of his cock perfectly visible through his pants. Even though I've never touched one before, I've got a general idea of what they're supposed to look like.

And this one looks *huge*, almost like the prince has a cucumber in his pants. Even as I push back against him, fucking myself with his hand, I can't stop staring at the thing.

"I asked you a question, kitten," he growls, and I finally tear my eyes away, taking his fingers in again as deep as I can.

"Yes," I moan.

He slides his hand along the outline of his clothed cock, smirking. I push back against his hand again and then gasp in surprise as he pushes another finger inside me, stretching my virgin entrance a little bit further.

"You're so fucking wet and tight," he says, his hand still tracing the outline of his cock, right in front of my face. I push back against him, sinking his fingers as deep as they'll go, and I moan even louder than before.

I keep going, faster and faster, while heat builds inside me. I've gotten myself off before, but never *this* way, and it's new and exciting and just completely incredible. I don't care that I'm on my hands and knees on a couch with someone I barely know, this just feels so *right* and so *good* that I'm powerless to stop.

"Grayson," I moan, trying to push him deeper. "Make me come again."

He chuckles, but I swear his cock practically jumps in his pants.

But then he pulls his fingers from my pussy, lazily running them against my clit before stepping around me,

Now he's right in front of me, and he inserts his fingers into his mouth one by one, licking them clean as I watch, fascinated.

"You're fucking delicious, kitten," he says.

I can't wait. I reach out for him with one hand, moving it slowly down his washboard abs to his belt, then slowly fingering the heavy buckle while I look up at him, biting my lip, like I'm asking for permission.

He chuckles again, then reaches down and slowly, excruciatingly slowly, undoes his belt. I'm panting for breath, and I can feel my juices running down the inside of one thigh.

Prince Grayson unbuttons his pants, unzips them, and I'm breathless with anticipation. I've never felt this way before, and I almost can't believe that I do now. It seems completely crazy, but right now, this is *all* I want.

Like I've been waiting my whole life for this moment.

Suddenly his cock springs free, and my eyes widen in shock. It's even bigger than it looked, and now I'm absolutely *certain* that this isn't what most penises look like. It's hard as a rock, throbbing, the tip shiny and a deep pink.

"Oh!" I say, because I can't think of anything else.

Grayson just chuckles and strokes it once, from the root to the tip and back, and suddenly I can't help myself. It's right in front of my face so I just open my mouth and close my lips around the shiny, swollen head.

The prince groans out loud, his hand still on the

base. Slowly, I swirl my tongue around it, and I can feel the tremor move through his body as I do, finally tracing my way up the veins running along the bottom.

"That feels so fucking good, kitten," he growls. "Look up at me. I want to see you with my cock in your mouth."

I take a deep breath, then push my lips down his shaft slowly, glancing up at him, and then take the base of his cock in my fist. He hits the back of my mouth before I'm even halfway down his shaft and I pull back slowly, licking and sucking the best that I can even though I've never done this before.

Grayson's hand rests on my head, and from the sounds he's making I seem to be doing okay as he pushes me back down, his hand insistent but gentle. I keep going, back and forth, up and down.

And I fucking love it. I love the noises that Grayson is making, I love having his thick cock in my mouth, and I love giving him pleasure like he gave me. Just knowing that he's inside me *somehow* is making me wetter than ever, my pussy aching with heat.

Finally, he growls, then grabs my hair and pulls my head back so that my lips are just barely around the tip. I swirl my tongue and suck a drop of salty precum from him, then look up.

"Kitten," he says, his voice deep and commanding. "I'm going to fuck you now."

Chapter Twenty

Grayson

Taking my cock out of Ella's mouth is one of the most impossible things I've ever done, but I have to.

I *need* to fuck her right now, feel her tight little pussy stretch around my thick shaft. I need to be the first man inside her, and I need to make her come until her toes curl.

"Please," she moans, her hand still wrapped around the base of my cock.

In one quick move, I flip her onto her back, move around the couch, and then I'm on top of her. I meld my mouth to hers, our tastes mingling, and even though her lips are slightly musky, I *like* it.

I've claimed her there. I'm going to claim her everywhere, in every hole.

Ella wiggles on the couch, wide-eyed, and I kneel between her soft, supple thighs, tossing one of her legs over the back of the couch. With one hand, I tease her clit again, slippery and sticky from her juices, then move it to her nipple, using it as lube to slide my fingers around her while she moans.

"Grayson, I need you *now*," she moans. "Please. I want you to be my first."

My cock throbs, and I grab it by the base, sliding the very tip between her slick, wet lips. I know I'm fucking huge, and I want to make her scream in pleasure, not pain. Ella arches her back, eyes closed, like she's trying to get me inside her, but I don't let her. Not yet.

Instead I push the head up, along her slit, until I'm teasing her pink little clit with it, then slide my length along her.

Ella whimpers, throwing her head back, and reaches down, taking my cock in her hand and pushing it against herself. It's so sexy that I hold my breath, just watching my cock touching her while she moans and writhes, completely and utterly *ready* for me.

I tease her clit a few more times while she bucks against me, breathless and wordless, and finally I position my cock at her entrance again. I'm totally bare, my skin against hers, and I *always* use a condom but I can't handle the thought of putting one on for Ella.

No. I need to be inside her, primal and raw. I need to fill her up completely.

"Grayson," she says again, her voice a ragged whisper, and that's all it takes.

Slowly, I push the head of my cock inside Ella, and she gasps. Her hands claw at the couch below her, and I grit my teeth. She's so tight, the tightest thing I've ever felt, and I can feel her sweet little cunt stretching around me as I enter her slowly.

I don't stop, but I pause for a moment, drawing myself out before I thrust in a little deeper, trying to get her used to taking my thick shaft as her pussy clenches and relaxes around me, Ella's breathing growing ragged.

"Touch yourself," I say, reaching up to tweak a nipple. "Show me how you touch yourself, kitten."

She looks at me in surprise for a moment, then reaches down with one hand and starts slowly circling her clit with two fingers, biting her lip as she does.

Just the sight of Ella, mouth open and face flushed, rubbing herself with my cock halfway inside her, is enough to make my balls clench, and I have to take a deep breath and pause for a moment.

"Don't stop," she murmurs, her eyelids at half-mast. "Please, Grayson."

She's so tight that even though I want to sink myself inside her, all the way to the hilt, I can't. I have to go slowly, give her time to stretch out and accommodate my girth. With every thrust she gasps and moans, still rubbing her clit, and she's looking at me with her eyes glazed by pleasure and lust.

"You've got a tight little pussy, kitten," I groan, still fucking her slowly. "You like feeling me stretch you out and fill you up?"

Ella doesn't answer, just moans as I slide deeper and deeper, rubbing herself harder and harder.

With one final thrust I finally hilt myself inside her and now Ella whimpers, thrashing her head to one side, her lip still between her teeth.

I grab her hips and pull her toward me as hard as I can, because I *need* every millimeter of my cock inside her as I bend over, my lips close to her ear.

"How does it feel to take my cock as deep as you can?" I ask, and bite her earlobe.

"Good," she gasps, her hips bucking and writhing. "Grayson, it feels so fucking good when you're inside me."

"You feel that?" I growl, grinding my hips into hers and moving my cock inside her.

Ella cries out, her back arching in ecstasy.

"That means you're *mine*, kitten," I go on, sliding out an inch and thrusting into her again, the sensation so strong that my balls clench again. "I'm claiming you as mine, right here, right now."

"I'm yours," she whispers. "Grayson, don't stop, *please*. I need this. I need *you*."

I thrust into her again, harder than before, and she cries out even louder.

"Yes!" she half-shouts, half-moans.

"Your sweet little pussy is mine," I whisper, then fuck her again. "Your mouth is mine."

I thrust again, each one harder than the last, and Ella's eyes are nearly rolling back into her head.

"Your pretty little tits are mine," I say, tweaking a nipple. "You're all mine, kitten."

She gasps as I slam into her, but now I'm fucking her too hard for words. Ella winds her hands around my shoulders, into my hair, and now she's just babbling in a steady stream: *please God yes Grayson fuck me Grayson I'm yours*.

"Come for me," I growl. "I can't last long in your pussy like this, Ella."

I don't even know if she hears me, but just as I say that, her eyes roll back in her head.

"Grayson!" she shouts, and then the walls of her pussy clamp down around my cock.

Ella arches and shouts, her entire body shuddering at once, her face flushed and her mouth open. It's the most beautiful thing I've ever seen, and I fuck her even harder as she comes, her pussy practically milking me but I grit my teeth and force myself to hold out.

This is her first time. Ladies always come first, but that's especially true right now.

Finally, she relaxes a little, her eyes still closed. I'm still hard inside her and I kiss her, nearly trembling from the force of not coming.

She bites my bottom lip as I pull back, then whispers, "Grayson, I want you to come inside me."

My hands clench on her hips, and I nearly orgasm in that instant.

"Bare?" I whisper.

Ella nods.

"Please?" she whispers, and I lose control.

I come so hard I shout, my head on her shoulder, bottoming out again and again as our hips slap together and I spurt again and again inside Ella, as deep as I can get. For some reason, the thought that we could be making a baby *right now* only makes me come harder, until it's finally over, and I lay on top of her, panting for breath.

At last, I push myself up and kiss her. She kisses me back fiercely, her tongue in my mouth, and when I pull back, she smiles.

"I'm yours," she whispers.

I drag one finger down her naked body, slowly going soft inside her.

"And I'm yours," I murmur.

Chapter Twenty-One

Ella

I know I have to get up and leave. Grayson probably needs to go back to the ball and put in one final appearance, and I know that Slade and Peyton will be home soon. If I'm not there, it'll just raise questions about where I am, and I'm not exactly looking forward to answering those.

Slowly, the Prince rolls off of me, and we both sit up on the couch. I run one hand through my hair and glance at him, suddenly feeling shy.

"I should go," I murmur, looking down.

"Stay," he says, sitting back against the couch and pulling me against him.

"I can't."

"I'm ordering you as the Prince," he says, and smiles at me rakishly.

My heart skips a beat, and for a second, I consider telling him everything: why I can't stay, how I'm an indentured servant to my stepmother and stepsisters, how I wasn't even supposed to be at this ball in the first place.

But I don't. Instead I snuggle against him, warm and hard and reassuring. After a little while he picks me up and puts me in his bed, but instead of going to sleep we fuck again.

The first time hurt a little when he entered me, but this time it doesn't at all. I just scream his name over and over again into a pillow, and seconds later, he unloads inside me.

· · ·

When I wake up I don't know where I am, and I sit bolt upright in bed, panicked.

Then there's a low grumble next to me, Prince Grayson stirs in his sleep, and everything comes rushing back: I'm still in the castle, in his bed. The bedside clock says it's 6:30 in the morning, and I relax a little.

Livia, Peyton, and Slade are never up before eight at the very earliest — often closer to nine. I've got the afternoon shift at the diner today, and that means a little time before I have to leave.

I lie back down, intending to go back to sleep, but something catches my eyes. Something *big*, tenting up right in the middle of the bed, and I bite my lip, then glance at the prince.

Sound asleep.

I shouldn't. I know it's dirty and wicked, but heat surges downward through my body and suddenly I'm not sure I can help myself. My pussy twitches with the mere memory of Grayson's monster cock inside me, and instantly my whole body flushes.

I think I might be addicted. I've never done anything like this before, not even close, but I just can't help it with him. I gave him everything last night and I want to give him even more.

I want to give Grayson pleasure in every way I possibly can, and I hardly even know him. Maybe I'm losing my mind.

But losing my mind or not, I pull the sheet off of his perfect body slowly, practically drooling at the sharp, rigid lines of his muscles. I'm already so wet I'm practically dripping with need as I remove the white sheet from his beautiful cock.

For a moment, I just sit there and admire it. Even though I'd never seen one in person before last night, I'm pretty sure that this is a particularly glorious specimen, long and thick, angled upward just the tiniest bit.

As quietly and gently as I can, I kneel over Grayson's hips and grab his cock in my hand. Instantly, he shifts in his sleep, though he doesn't wake up just yet as I stroke him carefully. My pussy is throbbing and aching already, and he's hard as steel in my hand.

I'm going to wake him up *right*, I decide. I've never done this before, but I understand the mechanics pretty well. I raise myself up on my knees, and even though I wobble a little, after a moment I've got his cock at my needy entrance and I'm biting my lip in sheer anticipation.

Grayson's eyelids flutter, and I pause, moving my hips back and forth gently, working the head of his cock against my entrance. Even *that* feels so good that I gasp, my hands moving to my own breasts, pinching my nipples.

Then, just as he opens his eyes, I lower myself all the way onto him with a single stroke, gasping as he fills me completely. Instantly, he grabs onto my hips, his hard abs flexing.

Slowly, I start riding him. I'm a little unsteady at first, and I put one hand on his chest to keep my balance, but his strong hands guide me. Soon I'm bouncing up and down, my mind slowly breaking into a thousand pieces with sheer pleasure.

Neither of us says anything. I can't even think of words right now, not as Grayson hits that sweet spot again and again that makes me feel like I'm spiraling upward, getting closer and closer to the sun. I pinch my own nipples even harder, gasping and moaning.

This feels dirty as hell, and I'm *not* this kind of girl — I'm a diner waitress who's just trying to get by — but I don't care, because right now this feels *so* fucking good.

I keep bouncing on Grayson's cock as I come, gasping out his name as he growls and pulls me down onto him, his cock so deep inside me I feel like I can barely even breathe. Seconds later I can feel him burst inside me and I bite my lip, savoring the feeling.

Grayson throws his head back against the pillows, his whole body rigid and tight with the force of his orgasm. He's completely stunning, not to mention oddly beautiful. I don't know why, but I have the feeling that not many people have seen him like this — in the throes of total and complete pleasure, first thing in the morning.

Strangely *vulnerable* like this.

When he finishes, I bend over slowly, my blonde hair dragging along his chest. He smiles as he looks up at me, his hands sliding up and down my body.

"Good morning," I say.

"That was the best wake-up call I've ever had," he grins, and then he kisses me.

Chapter Twenty-Two

Grayson

Ella's a drug. I got my very first hit when I saw her that hungover morning in the diner, and I've been addicted ever since.

And right now, instead of getting what I want and getting bored, I can feel my addiction, my *obsession* blossoming, something that's never happened before. I've never wanted a girl *more* once I've already had her, but with Ella I do.

I want to stay in my bed all day with her. I want to fuck her with her head thrown back on the pillows. I want to lick her soft, sweet pussy until she screams, and I want her pretty lips wrapped around my cock again as she swallows my load.

And between rounds, when we're too tired to move? I want to hear her laugh. I want her to tell me about life in my kingdom, the kind of life I've never been able to have myself because I've been busy being the Prince.

Ella slides off of me, and I spoon her again, pulling her into my arms.

"I should go soon," she murmurs again.

"What part of *I'm ordering you to stay* don't you understand?" I tease, running my fingers over one still-stiff nipple.

Ella just laughs softly, and soon, I'm asleep again. I've been a heavy sleeper my whole life — which is useful when your primary sleep hours are ten in the morning until five at night — and I fall into a deep, dreamless sleep where the only thing I really know is that Ella's in my arms.

When I wake up, I've rolled over, and I'm facing the other direction. I stretch sleepily, eyes still closed, and think about what I'm about to feast my eyes on: Ella, naked, ready, and inviting, and I roll over.

My bed's empty.

I blink. That can't be right, Ella was here maybe an hour ago. I woke up to her on top of me, sliding my cock into her, my voracious little kitten.

But she's gone. She's really not here, and for a horrifying second, I'm afraid I dreamed the whole thing. Maybe I've been so desperate to find this girl that I just invented last night out of thin air and I'm losing my mind.

Horrified, I stand up, still half-wrapped in the sheets, searching for something, *anything*, a clue that I'm not crazy.

And I nearly trip right over it, next to the door. A pair of high, crystal-studded shoes half-hidden under a chair. They sparkle in the light. I didn't notice her shoes, really, but now that I think about it there was a certain glimmer to her walk.

They have to be hers.

Her name was Ella. She works at a diner, and that's all I know about her — besides the fact that last night was the best night of my life, and I *need* her like a fish needs water.

I don't know why she left, but I keep thinking about her saying that she needed to go, like she was in trouble. Like she was *frightened* of something, and the thought alone makes a hard, black knot of fury tighten inside me.

I think Ella might be in trouble, and she didn't want to tell me. I clench her shoe in my hand and look toward the window where the sun's now up, and I make a promise: to me, to her, to the world at large.

Whatever's happening, I'll find you again.

Chapter Twenty-Three

Ella

I pay the taxi my last seventeen dollars, and the man drives off without another word. My father's mansion is in front of me, massive and stone with ivy crawling up the walls.

For a fleeting moment, I miss him again. I think of how, after my mom died and before he married Livia, it was just the two of us. Sometimes we'd eat spaghetti with ketchup for dinner, watching TV. I know he wasn't the perfect parent, but as I've gotten older I've realized that he was just trying to do his best in the wake of my mom's death.

But I sigh, shake my head, and make my way toward the house. I'm barefoot, but the grass is soft between my toes. I don't know how I'm going to get Thomas's friend's shoes back to him, but I'll have to find a way.

The gate clicks softly toward me, and I let myself in through the door to the servants' quarters, holding my

breath. I know that *if* the three of them are awake —
and, God forbid, if they've noticed I'm missing —
there could be hell to pay, but I'm honestly not
worried. I've still got plenty of time to change, shower
quickly, then make them coffee and breakfast before
they have any idea that anything happened.

As I walk down the hall, holding my torn dress
together with one hand, I think one last time about
turning around and going back. Maybe if I told
Grayson everything he would help me. After all, last
night was *amazing*, and that must mean something—
right?

I roll my eyes at myself.

Everyone knows about Prince Grayson, I think. *The
moment you wanted to do something besides have sex, he'd get
bored and start looking for someone else.*

*Better to leave on your own terms, like you did, rather than
have him kick you out unceremoniously.*

Last night was amazing — better than amazing —
but there's no way it can happen again. This is my real
life, and that was fantasy.

With a sigh, I push my bedroom door open, already
running down the list of what I have to do that day —
breakfast, wash the floors, laundry and ironing, dust
the sitting room — but then I stop in my tracks, the
list fading instantly from mind in shock.

I just stand there, my bedroom door half open,
totally frozen.

Run, I think. *Maybe you can just run and this will work.*

But I don't. I'm like a deer in the headlights, and
besides, where would I run?

"Good morning, Ella," says Livia from the chair
she's sitting in, her hair pulled back, her eyes ice chips.
"Late night?"

Chapter Twenty-Four

Grayson

"What do you mean, you *lost* her?" my father thunders. We're in the throne room, though it's empty except for us, and his voice echoes through the vast, empty space.

"I mean, she left, and I don't..."

I trail off, frustrated. I already feel like an idiot for not even knowing her last name, but I have this urgent, pressing fear that something in Ella's life is *wrong*.

That she needs me, and I'm standing here, arguing with my father.

"I didn't get her contact information," I finish lamely.

My father just glares, his arms folded across his chest. We're standing behind the thrones, stained glass windows throwing blotches of colored light across us.

"You disappear from the ball with a *commoner* that no one knows, you don't bother to come back, and now you're telling me you don't know who she is or how to reach her?"

He stalks to the other end of the dais, looking out at the vast room.

"You know, Grayson, a smart man might not believe you right now," he says, too angry to turn and look at me. "A smart man might think that you're trying to pull one over on him so you can have a few more weeks of whoring around with every floozy in the kingdom."

"Father, I'm not, I *swear*," I say, my voice almost pleading. "It's not what you think. Ella is different, she's special, she's—"

I stop short, because I can't even put it into words how I feel about her. I barely know her, but I know I'd go to the ends of the earth to find and protect her.

Slowly, my father turns. He gives me a long, hard look, his hands clasped behind his back. I stand my ground, even though he's the only person in the entire kingdom who has any sort of power over me.

"I'll make you a deal," he finally says, his eyes boring into mine.

I straighten, meeting his gaze squarely.

"What's that?"

"If I divert kingdom resources to help you find her, you marry this girl. Assuming she says yes."

Ten days ago, the mere thought would have made me nauseous. I'd have laughed in my father's face at the idea, but now — after last night, after my wild urge to put a baby in Ella's belly, to make her mine *forever* — it doesn't faze me at all.

Actually, I kind of like the idea.

"All right," I say. "If we find her, I'll marry her."

My father doesn't respond, just lifts one eyebrow.

• • •

"Shoes," my sister Aurora says. "You have shoes."

She doesn't sound impressed. I sigh.

"The chief inspector said he thought they looked custom," I say, slouching back on my couch.

We're sitting in one of the palace's TV lounges, this one only for the royal family and their guests. Some show is playing on the TV, but instead, I'm trying to tell my sister about what's happening.

"You have a custom shoe, then," Aurora deadpans. "Can't be many of those in a city of several million."

"It's all I have!" I nearly shout. "I've got her first name and her shoes. I didn't get her last name, her phone number, her address."

"Maybe she'll contact you," Aurora suggests, always reasonable.

I sigh again and run one hand through my hair.

"I think she's in trouble," I mutter.

Aurora looks at me.

"What?"

"I think there's something wrong," I say. "I don't know, she was... a little weird a few times, like something was off."

"Or this mystery girl you boned last night is a little weird," Aurora says, shrugging. "At least you're smart enough to wrap it up."

I go dead silent.

"Grayson."

I can't even meet Aurora's eyes.

"Did you—"

She stops suddenly, looking around the room.

"Did you fuck some crazy nameless girl *without a condom*?"

"She's probably on the pill or something," I mutter.

"Oh my god," Aurora says, covering her face with

111

both hands. "Oh my God. You're going to have a bastard. It's gonna fuck up the line of succession, you moron, there's gonna be a civil war in fifty years and it's gonna be because the legendary Idiot King Grayson the First boned a crazy chick."

I don't even have it in me to argue with Aurora. My little sister has always been the reasonable one, the one who was studious and smart in school, my solid rock through my wild life. When she was in a coma after a car accident a couple of years ago, I was a total mess until she woke up, but she did — miraculously unharmed.

"It'll be fine," I say. "I just... I just need to find her, Aurora."

Her face softens, even though she rolls her eyes a little.

"Well, don't take this the wrong way, but I'd start by taking those shoes to strip joints," she says.

I raise my eyebrows at her, opening my mouth, but she holds up one hand.

"I don't want to insinuate anything, but have you looked at them? Look at them. Those aren't regular people shoes. Just trust me."

I heave yet another sigh, and stand up.

"I do," I say. "Thanks, Rory."

She makes a face as I leave, because she hates it when I call her Rory.

Chapter Twenty-Five

Ella

Two Weeks Later

I open the fridge, grab the pitcher of margaritas, and pour Slade another one. My monitoring bracelet clanks against my ankle as I walk, a constant, heavy reminder of what's happened.

Livia happened. That's what. When I came home that morning, she *knew*. She saw me at the ball and she watched me disappear with the Prince and never come back, and she was *furious*.

She screamed that she owned me, that I was common dirt and not fit for royalty, that all I was good for was cooking and cleaning. She told me I'd never amount to anything, I'd never get out of her house, and my debt would never be repaid.

Then, to add insult to injury, she put this anklet on me. It's for house arrest, but she's either paid off or fucked half the police department, so two officers stood there and watched while she put it on me.

There was no escape. There's never been any escape.

Slade doesn't even look at me when I deliver her the margarita, just keeps her eyes closed as she bakes in the sun. I can practically smell her roasting.

I'm no sooner back in the kitchen than the doorbell rings, and I blink in surprise. We hardly ever have visitors — it's not like these three are capable of close friendships — so I hesitate a moment before moving toward the front door to answer it.

Seconds later, Livia pushes past me, turning as she walks.

"Ella," she commands. "Basement. *Now.*"

I hesitate, thinking that maybe she'll bustle off without waiting for me to hide, and I can stay near. Maybe it's Flynn, wondering where I've been for two weeks. It could even be cops that Livia *hasn't* paid off, looking for me.

But she stands there, glaring, and I head to the basement door, walk down a few of the creaky wooden stairs, and shut it behind me, sitting down so I can listen at the door.

There are two people, it sounds like, and I *think* they're both men but it's hard to tell. The front door is pretty far from the basement door, so sound is muffled at best and obliterated at worst. It takes them a while, but eventually they seem to leave. I don't hear their car drive away — too far, I guess — but after a long time, the door opens.

For some reason, I get my hopes up, that maybe they arrested Livia and now it's the police or maybe even Grayson himself coming to rescue me.

But it's not. It's her, glaring icy daggers at me, like I've done something to upset her just by sitting here in the dark.

"Come out," she snaps, and I walk up the few stairs again, not even bothering to look at her.

"The chandelier needs to be cleaned before you go to bed tonight," she says, her voice hard-edged.

I just close my eyes and don't respond. The chandelier takes me *hours* to clean, it's already the late afternoon, and I have to make dinner.

"Okay," I say, my voice listless.

Whatever her problem is, she's won. I had one night of fun, and now apparently, I'll be paying for it forever.

But it's okay. It was worth it.

Chapter Twenty-Six

Grayson

Another Week Later

The Chief Investigator, Jacques, pulls into the parking lot of the Hot Lips Lounge with me in the passenger seat. It's late afternoon, late enough for the performers to be there but not late enough for it to be crowded.

"You ready for this?" Jacques asks, sounding tired and weary. He didn't sound like that when we were going to strip club after strip club, searching for the owner of these shoes.

I'm *positive* that Ella was born female, but I'm grasping at straws. Maybe a drag queen at least knows something.

"Let's do this," I say, and we get out of the car.

At the front door, we're greeted by a drag queen whose heavily made up eyes instantly go wide when she sees us. I don't even have to introduce myself, she just curtsies almost to the ground, despite her high heels.

I'm kind of impressed. Those things look dangerous. Jacques holds up a shoe.

"Would you happen to have any idea whether these belong to a performer here?" he asks, his voice flat.

She purses her lips.

"They sure could. A little small for a queen, though."

The drag queen looks me up and down, then bats her eyelashes.

"Want to come backstage and ask around, sweetie? I'm sure they'd *love* to see you."

Jacques opens his mouth, and I can tell he's going to say *no* so I step in front of him, cutting him off.

"Yes, absolutely," I say, and we follow her to the back of the club.

• • •

"These might be Madeline's," says Minx July, a saucy redhead in a shimmering purple dress. "She's got tiny little feet. Hey, Madeline! Girl, are these yours?"

A small, raven-haired queen in a short green dress sashays over, and when she sees the shoes, her face lights up.

"Yes, they *are*, where on earth have these beauties been? I swear I let Charlize borrow them a couple of weeks ago and that whore never gave them back—"

"Who's Charlize?" I cut in, my heart suddenly pounding. It's the first good news we've gotten since we started searching, the first time *anyone's* had a clue about these shoes.

"She's our weekend headliner," Madeline says, giving me back the shoe and tilting her head. "Come on, she's this way."

Charlize is an Amazon in a blonde wig carefully dabbing lipstick on with a delicate brush, if drag queens can be Amazons. She turns to us when we walk up to her.

"Oh my Jesus," she says, and curtsies. "Your Highness, I had no idea you were going to be here tonight."

"I'm afraid we're not here for the show," I say, my whole body finally vibrating with excitement.

We're close. I can feel it. After weeks of having no luck at all, of thinking that maybe I'd lost my mind, we're *finally* close.

"Can I help you with something else?" Charlize asks, tilting her head to one side.

Jacques holds up the shoe, and Charlize gasps.

"You found that little tart!" she exclaims. "I borrowed those when I shouldn't have, and she got me into hot water with Madeline, let me tell you—"

"Ella?" I practically shout. "I *need* to find the girl who borrowed these, it's incredibly important. Please, if you can tell me *anything* at all."

Charlize looks surprised at my sudden outburst, and one hand drifts to her chest.

"Sweet little thing. She's a good friend of my boyfriend's, and she has this terrible stepmother who's basically enslaved her, and she needed an outfit for a ball..."

Her eyes widen, and I can practically see her putting two and two together.

"I met her at the ball," I say quietly. "She left without saying goodbye, and I've been looking for her ever since. I'd give anything to find her."

Charlize already has her phone out, dialing a number.

"Flynn, baby, it's me," she says, her voice surprisingly calm. "Prince Grayson is here asking about Ella. Think you can help?"

Chapter Twenty-Seven

Ella

I stare at the calendar hanging in the kitchen, chewing on the inside of my lip. I feel like an alligator has my insides in its jaws, and it's trying to crush me to death.

I'm pretty sure my period's a week late. I say *pretty sure* because I've never kept track all that well — it happened about once a month, everything always seemed normal, and I was definitely not getting pregnant, so I didn't bother.

Now I wish I had. I think I'd give almost anything to go back in time and *write down* when I started my last period, because I wish I knew whether I was giving myself an ulcer over nothing.

I try to tell myself that I'm remembering wrong, and it's just because of stress that I haven't gotten it yet. Stress is probably *also* why everything I've eaten in the last week has made me feel mildly nauseous, and why my breasts hurt so bad that rolling over wrong in bed wakes me up.

Getting pregnant your first time would be crazy, I tell myself. *What are the odds? Chill out.*

Not to mention that I'm terrified of what Livia might do to me if I were pregnant.

Speaking of the devil, she walks into the kitchen and stands imperiously in the doorway.

"Basement, *now*," she spits.

"Can't I just be quiet? Dinner will burn—"

"Was I unclear?" she snaps.

I turn off the burners on the stove, wiping my hands on a towel. She stands there, glaring at me, until she's interrupted by someone knocking on the door.

No. They're not knocking. They're *pounding* on the door. Even Livia jumps, and for once she actually looks shaken.

"Basement!" she orders, just as the pounding begins again. I put the towel down on the counter and walk toward the basement door, only to be interrupted.

"LIVIA TREMAINE, THE ROYAL GUARD DEMANDS THAT YOU OPEN THIS DOOR RIGHT NOW."

My mouth falls open and my heart leaps into my throat.

It's Grayson.

Livia turns pale, then bright red, and she marches toward me, her icy eyes narrowing.

"Get the *fuck* into that basement or I swear I'll—"

The pounding starts again, and now I can hear footsteps coming down the stairs like a drunk elephant.

"Jesus, Mom," Slade is saying. "Where the fuck is Ella, can't she do her job for once? I'm trying to sleep."

Livia whirls around, her eyes wide and panicked.

"Slade, *do not open*—"

The hinges creak.

"Huh?" Slade says.

"Where's Livia Tremaine?" Grayson barks.

Livia lunges for me, taking me totally by surprise. Before I can move she's grabbed me by the hair and yanks me backwards, nearly knocking me off my feet as she pulls me toward the basement door.

"Ow!" I yelp.

"ELLA!"

Feet stomp through the foyer. Slade makes an *oof* noise, and Livia just grits her teeth and drags me harder.

"I'm here!" I shout, my voice sounding strangled, my eyes burning with tears.

"Shut up, you stupid tramp," Livia growls as I put my hands around her wrist, trying to get her off of me.

I can feel my hair coming out by the roots, the pain white-hot and searing as I stumble backwards along the kitchen floor.

"Let me *go*!" I shout, and in that instant, the kitchen door bursts open.

Grayson's standing there, several uniformed men behind him. He doesn't say anything, but in three steps he's across the kitchen, and Livia lets me go just before he reaches her, and I stumble.

It doesn't matter.

"You're a fucking *monster*!" he shouts, and shoves her as hard as he can. She falls back against a wall, and it's the first time I've ever seen her look terrified.

Grayson advances toward her, a vein ticking in his forehead.

"I should beat you until you're as ugly on the outside as you are inside," he says, his voice low and dangerous. "I should—"

"Grayson," I say, both hands on my head, trying to make sure she didn't rip my scalp off.

He turns, and instantly, his face softens. I swallow hard, because there are tears streaming down my face and I have *no* idea what's happening.

"Ella," he murmurs, and the next thing I know he's wrapped me in his arms and I'm tight against his chest. "Ella, I'm so sorry it took me so long to find you."

I hug him back as hard as I can, burying my face in him, breathing in his scent — leather and stone, mixed with just a little bit of musk.

"What do you mean?" I whisper.

"You just left," he says. "And I didn't know your last name, where you lived, *anything*. I kept trying the diner, but since Livia owns it..."

The uniformed men are surrounding her now, and I can hear her pleading over their low, stern voices telling her that she's arrested for kidnapping, human trafficking, and a whole host of other things I can't make out.

"You were looking for me?" I ask, pulling back so we're face-to-face.

"Of course," he says, his eyes searching mine, and a small frown furrows his brow. "I told you I was yours, Ella. I meant it."

I have no idea what to say, but my eyes fill with tears again.

"I didn't think... I mean, I've read the papers, and..."

I bite my lip, because there's no good way to phrase *you've got a reputation for going through women like a hot knife through butter and I thought you were lying to me because of that* to the man who just spent three weeks tearing apart his own kingdom to find you.

But Grayson just grins, then kisses me gently, his lips soft and warm against mine. I kiss back greedily, hungrily, like he's a freshwater spring and I've been in the desert for weeks.

"That was all before you," he whispers when we pull away. "You changed everything, Ella."

The uniformed men take Livia away, out of the room. Peyton and Slade are screeching, so they're probably also in handcuffs, and for just an instant, I feel bad.

Then Grayson kisses me again, and I feel less bad. I let one hand drift to my belly, and I wonder if I should tell him.

Not yet, I think. *You're not even sure.*

Chapter Twenty-Eight

Grayson

She comes back with me. I insist on it. I've gone long enough without her, and I'm not letting her stay here, alone, in this enormous house that's haunted with memories of her evil stepmother.

The poor thing only brings two suitcases, and when I tell her that I'll send someone back for the rest, she just shrugs.

"This is just about it, actually," she says. "I mean, you can't pack up the garden or the birds."

When I drive her away in my limousine, she doesn't even look back, just leans her head against my shoulder and heaves a deep sigh.

• • •

Ella's pretty quiet the whole time, and I can't blame her. This has to be a huge shock, but the way that she kisses me every chance she gets, the way she slides her hands over my body and the way she *looks* at me says that she's glad I found her.

We install her in a suite in the palace next to mine, and the moment all her things are inside, I kick everyone else out. Ella stands in the middle of the ridiculously ornate room and looks around, wide-eyed and wondrous.

"You like it?" I ask.

Just watching her *standing* there is making me hard, so fucking hard I think I could cut glass with my dick. I've spent three weeks fantasizing about the night we spent together, about the way her eyes closed the first time I entered her, the way she looked over her shoulder at me an hour later as she eased onto my cock for a second time.

About waking up to her naked, sexy as fuck, and on top of me.

"It's different," she says, half-smiling. "I'm used to being around stuff like this, but I'm not used to living in it."

"This is yours now," I say, walking over to her.

I point at the couch, at the bed, at the floor, at the ceiling.

"These are all yours," I go on, taking one hand and lacing our fingers together, then putting both hands to my heart. "And *this* is yours."

Ella glances from my eyes to my lips, then kisses me. It's a deep, slow kiss, our tongues winding together as her body presses harder and harder against mine. I can practically feel her need, and I wrap my other hand around the back of her head, pulling her close.

Finally, she pulls back, her lips swollen and red from the kiss, her eyes heavy-lidded with desire and sparkling deviously.

That look alone makes my cock twitch and strain against my pants.

"What else is mine?" she asks, half-teasing, a smile playing around her lips.

Fuck, I love this side of her too, this good-girl-gone dirty that I'm completely powerless to resist.

I grin and move our hands lower, unlacing our fingers until her palm is flat against the outline of my cock in my pants, and I groan.

"*This* is yours," I growl, and her hand closes around me.

"Good," she says, and I capture her mouth with mine again.

I can barely hold back. Ella strokes me, and even through the layer of fabric heat sizzles through my body like I've grabbed onto a power line. I bite her lip and *growl* into her mouth, the sound pure and primal and *raw*.

I press my lips to her neck, biting and sucking on it as my hands grab her perfect tits through her dress and I pinch her nipples just a little bit harder than I should.

Ella gasps and whimpers, so I do it again. She trembles against me.

"Grayson," she whispers, and I take the shell of her ear between my teeth, licking it slowly.

"Kitten," I whisper. "I need you right fucking now, and right fucking here."

She squeezes my cock in response, and I groan into her ear.

"I've spent three weeks thinking about the way you say my name when you're about to come, and I can't wait any longer."

"Then don't," Ella murmurs, and her hand finds the zipper on my pants, pulling it down tooth by tooth.

I almost explode, but instead I pull up the skirt on

her work dress, grabbing her ass with both hands. I slide my fingers underneath her panties to find her soaking wet, and when I do she leans her head against my shoulder and sighs.

"You're wet as hell for me, kitten," I say.

"I know," she murmurs into my neck. "It's because I know what you're about to do."

I push my fingertips into her, feeling her writhe against my body. She takes my cock in her hands and it springs free of my pants, long and thick and so fucking hard I might never recover.

"I need you inside me," she whispers, stroking me from root to tip. It feels so good I shudder. "Please, Grayson."

That's all I can handle. I grab Ella by the shoulders and spin her around — not harshly, but not gently — and push her against the back of a couch, the closest furniture.

She yelps, then giggles as I shove her skirt up and yank her panties down to the ground, unbuttoning my pants and undoing my belt, giving my cock a little more freedom.

And I push myself against her, my thick cock hard between the round globes of her ass as she arches into me. Her hands dig into the fabric of the sofa and she sighs, turning her head to one side.

"I can't do gentle right now, Ella," I murmur into her ear as I grab the neckline of her dress and pull it down.

It tears. I don't care. I can buy her a new one.

"And I can't do romantic. Right now, I can only promise you hard and fast and fucking *deep*, but I can promise you that you're going to like it."

Her dress tears more, and she shrugs her shoulders out of it, now naked from the waist up, her skirt hiked to her hips. Ella undone like this is the sexiest thing I've ever seen in my life, at least until she reaches behind herself and grabs my cock again, leaning forward over the couch.

No; the sexiest thing I've ever seen in my life is Ella, bent over and undone, on her tiptoes, rubbing the head of my cock from her clit to her entrance, biting her lip and moaning.

I sink myself into her with a single stroke, and she cries out in sheer pleasure. I grab the back of the couch next to her hips and push myself into her as hard as I can as she arches her back.

"Grayson," she whimpers. "Fuck yes, Grayson."

I can barely breathe, she feels so fucking good. I'm inside her all the way to the hilt and her pussy is already fluttering and clenching around me, her hips moving as she bends over the couch, seemingly lost in a reverie of pleasure.

Scratch what I said before: Ella, gasping and moaning and flushed with my cock inside her is the sexiest thing I've ever seen.

I can barely hold out, and even though I *try* to go slow it's fucking impossible. Not when *this* is all I've thought about for weeks, not when Ella is moaning and gasping and whimpering.

Not when the only three words she seems to know are *harder, Grayson, please*. God, I love how filthy she gets when my cock is inside her.

I fuck her harder, holding her perfect tits in my hands, her nipples pinched between my fingers. It doesn't take long before she's reduced to gibberish, then just sounds, her back arched and her head thrown back.

It's a miracle that I don't come. It takes every ounce of self-control I have to fuck her like this and not come, but I'm a gentleman.

Just when I think I can't make it any longer, Ella grabs a handful of my hair in her fist and arches back, her chest heaving under my hands.

"I'm gonna come," she breathes. "Oh, fuck, Grayson, I'm gonna come so fucking—"

Ella screams, and it feels like a fist closes around my cock. I bury my nose in her hair and shout her name, because seconds later I explode like a nuclear bomb, coming hard and fast and long deep inside her.

I swear her whole body tightens at once, and Ella comes for *ages*, gasping and whimpering until she's finally done. She releases my hair and sags slightly against the couch, then looks back at me through her eyelashes.

Even though I'm still inside her, the look is somehow coy. Innocent.

And fucking hot.

"That what you needed?" I ask, tracing a finger down her sweaty spine as we both gasp for breath.

Ella just smiles and nods.

Chapter Twenty-Nine

Ella

I mean to shower, really I do, but instead Grayson hops over the back of the couch and before I know it he's grabbed me and flopped me over onto him. We stay there in silence for a long time, and I'm just reveling in being here, with him.

Okay, and a little bit in the memory of Livia being dragged away by the palace guard. I liked that too.

"Why didn't you tell me?" he murmurs after a long time.

We're half-sitting, half-lying, and we both got the rest of our clothes off so we're completely naked.

"Tell you what?"

"About your stepmother."

He's stroking my hair softly, and I stare at the ceiling, trying to put it into words.

"I just wanted to escape for a night," I finally say. "I didn't want to be some damsel in need of rescue. I wanted to have *fun* and not worry about her at all for a little while."

"I'd have helped you sooner," he says.

"I didn't know," I say, turning my face into his chest. "I thought that you said that stuff to all the girls, so..."

I trail off, not really sure what to say. He just keeps stroking my hair.

"That's over now," he says, his voice deep and sincere. "I haven't even thought about another girl in a month. Not since the day I saw you at the diner."

I blink, drumming my fingers against his chest.

Tell him, I think. *Tell him you're probably pregnant and see if he still says this romantic stuff then.*

"The day you wanted me to blow you in the bathroom?" I tease.

Grayson chuckles.

"If you want to know the truth, I think that would have ended with you on the counter and my tongue in your pussy," he says. "Even that day I could just *tell* you were fucking delicious, and hung over or not, I thought about my head between your thighs for *hours*."

My entire body blushes.

"Actually, can I ask you something?" he asks.

"What?"

He doesn't answer right away, just gets off the couch and rummages through a drawer for a moment. When he walks back, he's got something behind his back.

I frown.

And then Grayson gets down on one knee, both of us completely stark naked, and my mouth drops open.

"Ella Tremaine, I loved you from the second I saw you in that diner, and I've been trying to find you ever since," he says, pulling out a ring box from behind his back and opening it. "Will you marry me?"

I can't breathe. I can't move. I can't think anything except *oh no, oh no* over and over, because he doesn't know, and now I *have* to tell him.

"Ella?" he says softly, after a long pause.

I swallow hard.

"I have to tell you something first," I whisper, and Grayson frowns slightly.

"What?"

I close my eyes.

"I think I'm pregnant," I say in a rush. "My period's late, and everything makes me nauseous, so if that's not part of the deal then you can rethink or something because I know this is really sudden and unexpected, and—"

His hand caresses my cheek, and my eyes fly open.

Grayson's just staring at me, his eyes deep and serious, and I stop talking.

"Ella, are you serious?" he whispers.

I just nod, tears springing into my eyes.

He looks at me for another long, long moment.

And then he starts smiling.

"That's amazing," he says. "Are you sure? We have to make sure, we have to get you to the doctor and run tests and make sure that everything's okay. If that bitch Livia did something to you to hurt this baby, I swear I'll have her put to death."

I start laughing. I'm relieved and amazed, because I didn't think he'd be *excited*.

"I haven't even taken a pregnancy test yet," I say.

He's on his knees in front of the couch, and he grabs my thighs and pulls me forward until I'm practically lying in front of him.

Then he kisses my belly, right below my belly button.

"Hey," he says softly. "I'm your daddy. And I'm gonna marry your mom, and we're gonna live happily ever after."

He kisses my belly again, then looks up at me.

"If she agrees to it, anyway," he says, smiling and taking my hand.

"I agree," I say softly.

Grayson's still grinning, and he takes the ring from the box and slides it onto my ring finger.

"It fits perfectly," he says, and then there's a salacious sparkle in his eyes.

"It does."

"You know what else fits perfectly?" he asks, and kisses the inside of one thigh.

Heat bolts through me again, and I run my fingers through his hair.

"I think so, but we should try it just to make sure," I say.

• • •

Six Weeks Later

"I now pronounce you," the priest says solemnly. "Husband and wife. You may kiss the bride."

The entire throne room erupts into a cheer, thousands of voices all screaming at once, but they're drowned out by Grayson kissing me as my husband for the very first time.

He does it gently, tenderly. The perfect in-front-of-a-huge-audience first kiss.

But I know what's coming *later*. I know what he promised me last night as he slid into me as deep as he could, my knees over his shoulders, and my mind just about melted on the spot.

Tasteful kisses are for show. What happens in private is harder, rougher, and makes me come my brains out.

I'm practically in a trance as we walk back down the aisle, my enormous skirt swaying with every step. I can't believe we got married after the textbook definition of a whirlwind romance. I can't believe I'm a princess now, or that I'm growing our baby inside me.

It all seems so *surreal*, but then I look over at Grayson, he smiles down at me, and just like that, I'm sure.

Chapter Thirty

Grayson

Four Months Later

Flynn raises his eyebrows as I walk back into the kitchen. I was just here ten minutes ago, and he raised his eyebrows *then* when I asked for a bowl of ice cream and a bowl of Doritos.

"Let me guess," he says. "She didn't like them."

I clear my throat.

"Do you have any Cool Ranch Doritos?" I ask, trying not to smile. "The spicy ones are giving her heartburn."

Flynn rolls his eyes and tosses a hand towel over his shoulder dramatically.

"Those are the ones she wanted last week," he says, walking to the other end of the massive kitchen and opening a cupboard. "You sure it's the spice level and not the fact that she's *eating Doritos with ice cream?*"

I leave the two bowls in the sink and lean against the counter.

"Your guess is as good as mine," I admit. "I'm just the messenger, you know."

"I know," he says, pulling out a bag of Cool Ranch. "And you're a hell of a patient one, too. How's the nursery coming?"

"We're still deciding between lions and tigers," I say, grinning.

Flynn just laughs.

"Why not both?" he says, and hands me two bowls.

"I'll go suggest that," I say. "Thanks for the snacks."

"Tell that crazy pregnant lady to come see me if she can waddle down the stairs," he laughs.

"I'm not about to say the word *waddle* to her."

"Smart man," Flynn says, and winks before turning back to the bread dough he's kneading.

• • •

Ella and Thomas both turn when I open the nursery door. Thomas raises one eyebrow, but Ella just looks relieved.

"Thank you *so* much," she says, kissing me quickly. "I know it's really weird, but I swear I've been thinking about this for the past twenty-four hours."

She scoops up some ice cream with a Dorito and eats it. Her face says it's *bliss*. I don't question my seven-months-pregnant wife.

"Okay," she says around a mouthful. "Now we're thinking jaguars, since they actually live in the jungle. The whole room could be jungle-themed, you know, monkeys and birds and stuff?"

I step up to the table, looking at the things they've laid out. When I found out that when he's not Charlize,

Thomas is a sought-after interior decorator, I snapped him up *immediately*.

He and Flynn are two people I can never, ever repay, but I can give them their dream jobs.

"I did kind of like the savannah theme," I say. "Lions and elephants and giraffes."

Ella eats another chip with ice cream on it, thinking.

"We could do both," she suggests. "Unless you think that would confuse him, and then on his SATs he would say that lions live in India and never get into a good college."

"You're making fun of me again, aren't you?" I tease.

"I'm not the one who bought a copy of *Genius Babies* and reads it every night," she says, smiling.

Okay, maybe I've gone a little overboard. I *may* have read almost every book on pregnancy and childrearing I could find. I may have both the head of the pediatrics unit and the head of the gynecology unit on speed dial.

And I *may* have already ordered our unborn child a swing set that he won't even be able to use for two years, and Ella may not know about that one yet.

But I'm excited. Really, *really* excited to be a dad, and I can't help it. I've loved this kid since the moment Ella told me that she thought she was pregnant, and I love him more than I thought was possible.

"I think he'll figure out tigers and lions before he's seventeen," I say. "At least, he will if I follow *Genius Babies* to the letter."

Chapter Thirty-One

Ella

That night, standing in front of a mirror, I turn to the side and make a face, drawing my robe tight against my belly.

I'm only seven months, and I already look and feel like a *whale*. I swear I'm constantly bumping into things, hanging onto railings for dear life whenever I go up or down stairs, and rolling over in bed?

I told Grayson not to be surprised if one day he comes into our bedroom and I've hired a crane to do it for me.

The bathroom door opens and there he is, clad in nothing but boxers and a grin. *He* looks exactly the same of course — ripped abs, huge, tight muscles.

Thick pole standing at attention.

He walks up behind me, kissing my shoulder and caressing my belly. Instantly my nipples poke through the thin fabric of my robe, and he fondles one, kissing the back of my neck.

"Come to bed," he growls. "I've got something for you."

I lean back against his hard, sculpted chest, trying not to wobble since my balance isn't what it once was.

"What is it?" I ask.

His lips wander over the side of my neck as he unties the sash of my robe, letting it fall to the ground. He caresses my belly again, then slides his hands between my legs, finding my wetness.

"My cock," he says, his voice low and rough. "I'm afraid it's not very creative."

I just laugh, and in one movement he picks me up and carries me to the bed, putting me down gently and scooting me backward, his lips trailing over each nipple, then over my massive belly, my hips, then my thighs.

Then he tosses my knees over his shoulders and I can't see him anymore, since my belly's in the way, but then he licks me slow and hard from stem to stern, right across my aching lips and to my clit, and I clutch the bedsheets and moan.

Grayson licks faster, harder, his hands clutching at my thighs as he kneels next to the bed. I still feel like a beached whale, because I can't move and I'm just gasping for breath, but Grayson knows *exactly* what he's doing.

"Fuck, that feels good," I gasp.

He slides two fingers inside me, and my whole body tenses. He licks my clit even faster, crooking his fingers at the same time.

I'm primed to explode, and I can hear myself moaning as he keeps moving steadily and I spiral upward.

"Please," I breathe, because I know what he wants

to hear, what will drive him *crazy*. "Please, Grayson, make me come."

All at once he locks his lips around my clit, twists his fingers in my pussy, and I fly over the edge. I can't arch my back anymore, but I throw my head to one side and my fingers and toes all curl while I whimper.

The moment I'm done, Grayson pulls his fingers out and licks them off, crawling over me in bed.

"That's not the present you promised," I tease, still breathing hard, jolts still rocketing through my body.

Grayson just grins.

"I know," he says, and kisses me. "But sometimes I can't help giving you a teaser."

He kisses me again, caressing my belly, then moves away. I take a deep breath, and he offers his hand, helping me sit up and roll over.

It's not sexy. I'm *very* aware it's not sexy, but in a moment, I'm on my hands and knees, Grayson bent over me, my head turned for a kiss.

"You know you're hotter than ever with our baby inside you, don't you?" he murmurs, pinching one nipple.

I moan, my head back, and he runs his hand down my back to my slit, where he runs one fingers over my lips.

"I can barely control myself around you," he goes on, and now the hot head of his cock is pressed against my lips.

I rock back against it gently, just barely letting the head penetrate me, and sigh with my head thrown back. Grayson grabs my hips hard, but he doesn't push inside me.

He knows I need to go slow right now, that hard and fast just isn't what I *want* right now, for whatever reason. I rock back further, letting him slide in more and this time I moan.

I keep going until he's bottomed out inside me, and then I stay there for a moment, just loving the feel of his thick, long cock inside me. Every single time we fuck I'm surprised again at how *good* it feels, at how he fills me so perfectly.

Then he pulls back, slowly, and thrusts again. He goes slowly, but it's still hard and deep, and it's exactly what I want right now. In seconds I'm moaning and gasping, biting my lip and clawing at the bedsheets.

"You like that?" he growls, bottoming out again and again.

Somehow, I end up face down on a pillow, and Grayson grabs one shoulder.

"Just like that," I gasp. "Grayson, *please*, just like that."

He fucks me again and again just like that. I'm moaning into this pillow nonstop, my toes curling. I think I'm shouting his name over and over again along with the words *don't stop*, and it's a matter of seconds before the orgasm hits me like a tidal wave.

I scream. I whimper. I shout *fuck me, Grayson* into this pillow, and the moment I'm done I can feel that magnificent cock jerk inside me as he unloads, again and again while I gasp for breath.

He leans over me without pulling out, breathing hard, and kisses the back of my neck again. I turn my head.

"That was so good," I whisper.

He chuckles.

"Better get it in now before the baby comes," he says. "That six weeks is gonna be hard as hell."

He pulls out and we roll onto our sides, spooning. Grayson's hand drifts over my belly, again and again. The baby's kicking now, and I gently put his hand where Grayson can feel.

"I think we woke him up," I tease.

He snuggles in closer.

"You know how much I love you both, don't you?" he says. "To the stars and back."

The baby kicks, and I tear up.

Hormones, I'm sure.

"I love you too," I whisper. "And I know he does too."

"I'm so happy I found you," he whispers. "I'd have looked forever."

"I'm happy you found me too," I say.

We fall asleep that way, nestled together in bed, his hand protectively on my belly.

THE END

ABOUT PARKER GREY

I write obsessed, dominant, alpha heroes who stop at *nothing* to get their women - and get them dirty!

I can be found driving around my small, southern town in either my minivan or hubby's pickup truck. No one here is the wiser about my secret writing life… and I definitely prefer it that way!